The Chronicles of Bethica

The Rise of Bethica

Warren W. Randall Jr.

The Chronicles of Bethica

Warren W. Randall, Jr.

Universal Battles Books RPG

Alliance, Ohio 44601
Universalbattles.com
Realmofbethica.com

First published by Universal Battles Books RPG 2017

ISBN 978-0-9862928-4-2

Dedication

This book is dedicated to Fantasy Role Playing lovers everywhere.

Acknowledgment

I would like to thank my editor Harriett L. Randall for her fantastic contribution to my book. My appreciation also goes to the designer, rebecacovers who created my amazing book cover.

Special Appreciation

for

Diana L. Randall

My wonderful and beautiful wife for her love and understanding while I under took this project.

Table of Contents

Chapter One

The Call of Lord Abram

In the quiet dark of night, Lord Gangus Abram was awakened by a mysterious voice; his eyes flashed opened and darted back and forth across the bedroom ceiling. His hand tightened into a fist, and his heart raced. Gangus glanced over at his wife, Brehira, who had not stirred. He eased out of bed, tipped to the far side of the room and stood looking around nervously. The room had suddenly grown icy cold, and Gangus shivered in his thin bed clothes. "Who is there?" he whispered, with water vapor fogging out of his mouth after each word.

"Go quickly to the north end of the forest," a strange voice said. "There, you will find a single cottage. Speak to a man called Naman."

The voice was like no other Gangus had ever heard. It spoke like a gust of wind, yet the words were clear. It came from everywhere in the room, yet nowhere could he pinpoint its direction. He glanced once more over at Brehira who was still sleeping. Why couldn't she hear it? Had it done something to my sweet? He walked briskly over to the bed and touched her shoulder lightly. When she stirred, he blew out a grateful breath of air and pulled the covers over her shoulders. Brehira was the love of his life. He had married her when she was seventeen and brought her to this land called Volaria. With his great wealth, he built a manor house where Brehira bore him two sons, Khimah and Dinary.

Gangus had lived in this land all of his life. Volaria was a single land mass surrounded by the Endless Ocean. The Endless Ocean lived up to its name, for it stretched for hundreds of miles. Over the years, numerous captains who grew weary of its length with its hostel waters would often turn back.

Volaria also proved a genuine paradise because of the rich soil that yielded vegetables and fruit all year round; the waters overflowed with every kind of edible creature; plus, the weather was suitable for cattle and sheep farming.

Gangus was a magnificent man with olive skin and dark mixed gray hair. At six feet and still muscular for an ex-soldier of forty-eight, he was well respected and known as a man of great courage who remained obedient to the will of the gods. Tonight, Gangus wasn't sure if he could live up to that name. The voice had sent chills along his skin, yet he felt a strange sensation to obey. So, he dressed quietly, grabbed a lantern and tip toed past each son's room—down the long hall past the servant's quarters, down the spiraling staircase and out the door.

Under the dark, starry sky, the moon was full and unusually bright. When night birds flew in front of it in a 'Z' formation, Gangus felt something was about to happen; or had the incident just given him the creeps? Nonetheless, he picked up his pace as he walked along the grassy path, past the large, tall trees with its hooting owls and other creature songs of the night. The forest was thick and eerie. The top of the trees swayed back and forth with the rhythm of a gentle breeze.

After what seemed like thirty minutes of walking, Gangus arrived at the north end of the forest and spotted the lone cottage with a light shining through a thin curtain at the window. No one was usually awake at that hour, so he assumed he was expected him. Before he knocked, a voice called him by name from beyond the door. But this was the deep voice of a man. His hand hurtled to his side where he gripped the handle of his sword and stood staring at the door, hesitating to advance.

"Lord Abram," the voice called again.

"I am here," he answered forcefully to mask the fear in his voice.

Gangus strolled to the door and found it cracked. He laid his lantern aside, and with one hand still gripping his sword, he pushed the door open with the other. He entered the one room and found it dark, where a single candle sat in the middle of a small table near the window. From a dark corner, a shadowy figure spoke.

"Come into the light."

"Who are you?" Gangus asked with authority.

"I am the Oracle, Naman. I knew of your coming."

"How? Who told you?"

"He goes by many names, but you know him as Raziel God of Leadership and Honor among other titles," he said, his voice trailing off.

"Why should I believe you?"

The Oracle mentioned an incident that had taken place in Gangus' early life—something Gangus had never revealed to a living soul. Gangus stumbled backward but didn't speak. When he had gained his composure, he blurted, "What manner of sorcery is this?" Then he moved closer to the light.

8

"Not sorcery," Naman said, "I assure you." The Oracle motioned for him to sit. Gangus stepped forward and sat in front of the light. Then the Oracle came out of the shadow holding two tin cups. He placed the cups on the table and sat before Gangus.

Gangus saw that the Oracle was short and fair—more hair on his face than his head. He found him to be quite peaceful-looking for a man with such an overwhelming presence. And, he was blind.

"What did the Lord Raziel say to you concerning me?"

The Oracle reached from beneath his chair and brought up a jug. "Have some wine. You have come a long way. I am sure you could use a drink?" The Oracle didn't wait for an answer. He held the jug, placed his index finger in the tin cup and poured—his fingers measuring how far the wine came up to the rim without going over it. He handed the cup of wine to Gangus.

"Thank you," Gangus said.

Then the Oracle poured one for himself.

Both men took a hefty swallow. The Oracle felt around for Gangus' cup and half-filled it again before doing the same for himself. After both had their fill, the Oracle spoke.

"You have been given a great gift. The gods do not treat everyone so."

"Gods! There's more than one now? What is this gift?" Gangus asked taking another gulp.

"You will leave Volaria and go to a far off land which Raziel has already shown you, and from the loins of your sons will spring great kingdoms."

"That's the gift? If it is, Raziel can keep it," Gangus blurted, wine dribbling down his chin.

"Careful what you say." The Oracle's milky white eyes moved around in its useless sockets as if he feared someone else was listening.

Gangus' heart sank. "I am to leave my home. That does not make sense. Leave paradise and go where, to…to some distant land? And what about my family? What if I can't persuade them? What if they refuse to go? I'm not leaving them behind. No!" he said shaking his head. As he looked to the ceiling, he muttered, "Raziel, you asked too much." Gangus flopped back in the chair. He threw his head back and drained his cup of wine then slammed the empty cup down on the table.

"It is a hard, hard thing to ask any man. I know," the Oracle said. "But you, Lord Abram, are not just any man. I think you have known you were special since you were a boy." The Oracle slid a map across the table to him. Gangus unfolded the map and examined it. It was the most unusual map he'd ever seen.

Gangus' chest was hurting for what he was about to do to his family. But he knew it was the will of the gods. It was confirmation of all of the dreams he'd been having for the past three years, like dreams of a long journey across rough oceans, dreams of entering a distant and hustle land, and dreams of battling monsters. Dreams he had prayed were just the result of too much wine before bedtime. But now, he knew. Gangus took the map, folded it and stood to leave. He stopped and looked over his shoulder at the Oracle. "Thank you. I apologize for my reactions, for now, I know that only a god could have revealed this to you."

When he returned home and entered his bedroom, Brehira was sitting up in bed and had a look of fear and puzzlement on her face. He placed the lantern on the table and began taking off his clothes.

After a few minutes, she said, "Really? You have nothing to say?" She stared at him.

Gangus slid into bed beside her. "Not tonight," he said. He attempted to kiss her, but she leaned away. Brehira was still beautiful for a woman with two adult sons. She had long, dark hair and flashing dark brown eyes.

"Where were you? I...I thought something had happened."

"Sweetheart. I'll explain in the morning," he said pulling up the covers.

"In the morning? What was so important that you had to leave this time of night and say nothing to me? Do you know I was about to wake the others? Sound the alarm?"

He leaned in, she didn't move this time, and he kissed her lips tenderly. "Honey, please—in the morning. I've had a trying night." He rolled over on his side, facing her, and closed his eyes.

Brehira looked up to the ceiling in disgust. She blew out the light then looked over at her husband. She twice pounded her pillow seeming to get it just right for sleeping, but acting as if she wished it were his head. She lay back and went to sleep.

Just before dawn, Brehira woke and, again, found that her husband wasn't beside her. She grabbed a cloak as it was always a little chilly in the mornings and went into the family room where she found Gangus fully dressed—unusual for him that early, and standing peering out the window. He had a faraway look, and deep frowns lined his forehead.

He didn't hear her when she walked up beside him. She gently placed her soft, tan hand upon his shoulder. He turned and acknowledged her with a smile and a kiss on the cheek.

"What is it, my husband? What has troubled you so?"

"The gods have asked the unthinkable."

"Where did you go last night? Was that the god's doing?"

"I'm afraid so."

"But…but why?"

He placed his finger upon her plump lips and shushed her. "I'm going to call a meeting as soon as it's light. I'm going to tell everyone at the same time."

"But…why can't you tell me now. Can't you see I…?"

"Please, honey. Don't make me say this twice."

With that, he dragged off away from her and towards the bedroom.

"Then I'll make us tea," she told him.

He nodded and continued into the bedroom.

Later on in the day, in the large room set aside for celebrations, Brehira, Khimah, Dinary, the house servants, and many of his neighbors were helping themselves to lamb chops, salads, green vegetables, fruits, and brew. Then Abram stood and begged everyone's attention.

Khimah and Dinary were tall and well built like their father. Khimah was the oldest and was in his late twenties. He had fair skin and blue eyes. Dinary who was in his mid-twenties, had olive skin, dark hair, and eyes. Both were skilled in combat (trained by their father) and were considered by noblemen as ideal husbands for their daughters.

"My dear wife," Gangus began, "My sons, neighbors, and friends. I know this will come as a huge shock to you, but last night, the gods spoke to me through the Oracle Naman. Until last night, I thought my dreams of a journey were only foolish dreams. But now I know they weren't just dreams. The gods demand that I take my family and others who wish to travel with me to a new land across the Endless Ocean. The gods promised that we would find an even greater paradise."

Brehira gasped. Dinary was speechless. Eyes flashed up at him, and mumbling grew loud among the small crowd.

"Father! The gods?" Klimah said. "That makes no sense. Naman is no

11

Oracle—just a crazy old blind man who hears voices. He should be put away, going around ruining people's lives with this nonsense."

"Gangus, you...you can't be serious, love."

Dinary swallowed hard and found his voice. "Father, You are going to leave all this? Have you forgotten what we had to do to keep this land, all the battles we fought against those land-murderous Trolls, and thieving Goblins and Orcs?"

"No, son, I've not forgotten."

"Mother, talk to him," Dinary pleaded.

Brehira, regretting her duties as a wife, stared at Gangus, her eyes glassy and spoke half-heartedly. "Where my husband goes, I go," she said, her voice cracking; then she stormed out of the room.

"There, you see. Now, look what you're doing to Mother." Khimah said angrily. "How could you do this...make her leave her home, and for what, to travel to some godforsaken land across the Endless Ocean? It is called endless for a reason! All who have tried to sail it either returned years later with ocean madness or did not return at all."

"Khimah, listen...," Gangus said.

"No! I won't listen. I think you're foolish, Father." He turned to Dinary. "And you're an idiot if you follow him." Khimah stormed out of the room to console his mother.

"I believe you should think this over, Father," Dinary said before climbing the stairs to his bedroom.

Celio— medium height, dark haired man in his late thirties spoke up. "If you're set on going," he said, "I would love to join you on this journey, My Lord. Those of us who fought beside you would surely welcome the adventure."

"You mean, you'd leave all this?"

"All what?" he said, looking around him. "A lot of us ex-soldiers are restless. We miss the excitement. Why I never felt more alive than when we were fighting those smelly Trolls," Celio said, turning up his nose.

"Are you serious? You mean you'd go with me?"

"Sure. I know quite a few men who are as restless for excitement as I am. You'll need some extra swords if you insist on traveling to this strange land. Never know what trouble you might find."

"Well, what about your women?"

"Some, like me, have none and those that do, well, they are pretty much like your misses—if you pardon me for saying so, My Lord. They'll follow their men anywhere."

Gangus chuckled. "I would be proud to have you with me, Celio, and all the men you can muster up."

"Just let me know when you're ready to leave, My Lord."

"I will." Gangus turned to exit the room. "Stay as long as you like. There is plenty of food." He walked into the dining area where Khimah was trying to console his mother. Brehira looked up at Gangus with puffy eyes. Gangus sighed and looked down at the floor.

Chapter Two

The Necklace

"So, you *are* an idiot," Khimah said to Dinary.

"Come on, Khimah, give it a rest. We've been through this." Dinary folded a shirt and placed it in the trunk.

"I'll give it a rest when you and mother come to your senses."

"Look! I don't like this any more than you do. If you want to stay, Khimah, then stay. I'm not letting mother leave here without one of us going with her; and that's that," Dinary said slamming down the top of the trunk.

Khimah's face softened. He walked up to his brother and placed a hand on his shoulder. "Then...please, take care of her," he said quietly.

Dinary looked into his big brother's eyes. "You know I will...and we'll see each other again. I promise."

Khimah pulled his necklace over his head and placed it around Dinary's neck. It was made of fine metal—a silver eagle; its beak pointed left with one emerald eye and a sword as its tail.

Dinary looked up at his brother. "But I've never seen you without this. You once scolded me when we were children just for reaching out and touching it."

"It may someday bring you luck, my brother." Khimah grabbed and tightly hugged Dinary then quickly left the room.

The hour had arrived. There had been a big feast and fireworks the night before. All of the villagers had come out for the big send-off of the Abrams, their loyal servants, twenty ex-soldiers, and their wives.

There were tears and waves and children running beside the horses and carriages. Brehira couldn't stop waving at Khimah. She held a handkerchief to her runny nose the whole time, waving and throwing kisses his way—her cheeks wet. Dinary had to turn her around so she wouldn't strain her neck.

The ride was quiet. There was nothing left to do now but focus on the long journey that was ahead of them. When they reached the ship, the luggage was carried on by the servants, and everyone stood on the deck and waved to a few neighbors who had traveled to see them off. Khimah didn't want to come. He said he couldn't bear it.

Warren W. Randall, Jr.

Gangus and Brehira settled into a luxurious cabin for a two-day trip to the next port. There, they would board the ship for the Paradise journey. Dinary was next door. Gangus made sure all in his company, his servants as well as the soldiers who chose to travel with him, were in similar cabins. Brehira insisted on treating them no differently.

But not long after they had gotten into deep water, they ran into a terrible wind storm. Everyone was told by the captain to stay in their cabins. The wind tore through the waves as they crashed against the ship that rocked from side to side, throwing passengers from one end of their cabins to another.

The hours wore on. Gangus, now shut up within his cabin, began to worry. Next door, Dinary looked out of the window. In the dark, the tall waves looked like giant blue fish foaming at the mouth and jumping in and out of the ocean. The wind continued to whip as the temperature dipped suddenly. The dark clouds had covered the moon, and there seemed to be no stars in the night sky. As the ship tilted to one side, Dinary hung on to the furniture for dear life and quietly cursed his father for making them trade paradise for death at sea.

Then, as quickly as the storm had begun, it became quiet and calm. Gangus noticed it and opened the cabin to find people moving about in the halls. He and Brehira decided to join them after being shut up for hours. Brehira knocked on Dinary's door. He opened and peeked around before coming into the hallway.

"I thought we were going to die," he said joining them on the walk. But to Gangus' surprise, people weren't going on deck but assembling in the dining area to listen to the captain. As they stood among the crowd, they heard the captain say, "Ladies and gentlemen." But before he could say anything further, the people broke out into a loud cheer for how well the crew handled the ship during the storm.

The grateful captain smiled and motioned for everyone to be quiet. "I'm afraid that, although we managed the storm well enough, we've emerged off course and the fog seems to be thickening by the hour."

"What exactly are you trying to tell us?" Someone in the crowd yelled.

"Quite frankly, we have no idea where we are."

There was loud muffled conversation among the people. There were only a hundred aboard ship, not counting the crew.

"I promise you we are doing the best we can," the captain continued. "You

16

can travel outside your cabins but please not on deck. And dinner will be served at the ringing of the dinner bell. Thank you for your patience."

There was lots of mumbling as people filed out of the dining area. Gangus, Brehira, and Dinary strolled back to their cabins. Dinary decided to wait for the dinner signal with his parents. It was five o'clock.

While Gangus was reassuring Dinary that everything would be all right, Brehira who stood combing her hair and primping, gasped when a loud thud rocked the ship, throwing her into the wall with Gangus and Dinary tumbling after her.

"What was that?" she shouted, lying flat on her back.

"It feels like we hit something," Dinary said, helping his father to his feet.

"Help your mother. I'm going out to see what's going on." He opened the door, and it was pandemonium. People were yelling and running about hysterically. There was flooding in the halls and water pouring in from the ceilings. Gangus turned back to them. "Grab your mother; we've got to get off this ship."

"What's happening?" Dinary asked.

"We're sinking, that's what's happening. Come on; we have to go," Gangus said motioning to them to leave with him.

Brehira broke away from Dinary. "But my things—I'm not leaving my things," She grabbed several bags.

"No! Leave them," Gangus demanded. "They won't let them on the rowboat anyway."

"But…"

"Honey, come on, we're wasting time." She reluctantly dropped all the bags, but one—a carrying case with her jewels.

Gangus grabbed Brehira under her arm, and Dinary had her other. People were running into each other, falling; more water gushed out of the ceiling and from the right side of the ship. Gangus turned his head about looking for his servants and clansman. He spotted a few running towards him, headed by Celio. Gangus asked him where the others were.

"I don't know," Celio said. "Stay here; I'll see if I can find them."

Gangus and the others waited as long as they could but decided to leave when the water rose to their knees. Then Gangus told them they had to go.

Brehira looked at him. "What about the others?"

"They'll just have to find us."

As soon as they started up the staircase, Gangus heard Celio call. He looked back, and the rest of his clan were moving as fast as they could as the water was steadily rising. They joined Gangus, and all started up the stairs.

When they reached the deck, they were just in time to board the last remaining boat. The fog was so thick, they could barely see one another.

"Hold each other's hands," Dinary yelled. "And don't let go until we're all in the boat."

They held hands, and one by one climbed into the small boat. As the boat was being lowered down from the side of the ship, there was a loud cracking sound; the ship was going under while the boat was still attached to it.

Celio yelled. "Hold on!" The ship tilted forward. Celio stood on the edge of the boat, pulled out a small knife and feverishly sawed the ropes that connected the small boat to the ship.

"Hurry! Celio! Hurry!"

"I'm trying!"

The small boat tilted more, and everyone was holding on as tightly as possible. Brehira broke every finger nail as she gripped the side of the boat. And poor Celio continued to saw away as the boat continued to swing forward.

"What are you using, your teeth?" Dinary yelled.

Another loud crack and the boat hauled everyone forward.

"Jump!" Gangus shouted.

But Celio kept sawing away at the last piece.

"Let go, Celio, for god's sake, man jump!"

Dinary held on to Brehira, and he leaped from the boat. Gangus leaped, as did the others, and swam away from the boat as fast as they could before the ship created a whirl pool that would surely have them spiraling down with it. Blindly, they swam through the fog—staying close to each other by calling out. The water was cold. Something bumped Gangus' leg. A creature, coming to take a bite of him, he thought. Over and under, his arms smashed and lifted from the water as he swam through the fog. He thought he saw a massive creature jet pass him. He shot his head left and right, but saw nothing except the thick gray. He called out to his wife and son but got no answer.

Kicking as hard as he could, Gangus thought he saw a bright light breaking through the fog. He glared. He had seen it. He could barely make out shipmates in a row-boat, and one had a lantern waving it from side to side. Gangus yelled. "Brehira! Dinary! If you can hear me, swim to the light! Everyone swim to the light!"

Another thirty or forty strokes later, he reached the boat. The shipmate pulled the women into the boat. Then Dinary got in and helped Gangus who turned to help the rest of the men and women. As Gangus lay back shivering and blowing a great sigh, he looked around the boat then suddenly shot up into a sitting position. "Where's Celio?" he snapped. Everyone squinted, peering through the fog yelling his name and listening. But sadly, he didn't answer.

*****

As the quiet waves gently rocked the small boat, everyone lay sleeping. It was day break, and the sky was orange with the dawn rays of the sun. Large pale blue gills flew overhead; each diving into the ocean and flapping their wings as if they were bathing. Some were menacing, diving into the boat and pecking at the slumbering crew. Dinary woke and smacked at one. He sat straight up, yawned, and scratched his chest. His eyes were a bit blurry, and he tried to make out a dark object that was moving fast towards them. He blinked several times until his eyes were clear and gasped at what he saw.

He shook his father.

"Umm…what?" Gangus asked, sitting up.

Gangus rubbed his eyes then called to the others to wake up. Coming towards them was a ship. Men were waving frantically at them. The others in the small boat were wide awake now, sitting up and waving back at the men like crazy. When the ship got closer, they let out a loud cheer.

One of the men from the ship yelled, "Ahoy there!"

Gangus blinked, widened his eyes, and said, "Celio?"

Chapter Three

Pirate Ship

Traveling in the company of a ship's captain who had a huge bounty on his head was not something Gangus had anticipated. However, Captain Orroh, or as he was affectionately called by his mates, Captain Orr, was sailing west towards Skatts Island. There, Gangus could use Brehira's jewels to finance a large ship with an experienced captain and crew, who would take them to their destination. But first, he would need clothes, food, and lodging for the sixty people who came with him.

"Sir," one of the shipmates said. "Lady Abram asked that I fetch you. We put her in the cabin next to the captain's. I'll take you there, sir."

Gangus nodded and placed his mug of hot tea aside. He stood, tightening the blanket around his shoulders and followed the man whose name was Khomo.

Down a loose-board staircase, then a narrow, dim hallway—Gangus lagged behind, his eyes taking in the appalling view. If the smell wasn't bad enough, three very large rats met them in the hall and didn't look too intimidated when the men's feet clunked towards them. Khomo had to kick at one before they all scurried into an oval hole. The man stopped. "Here, sir," he said to Gangus while pointing to the cabin door.

Gangus thanked him and opened the door to a pouting Brehira who was facing a portrait of an exotic princess, with chocolate bare breasts and charcoal nipples. "Disgusting," she said turning away from it and facing Gangus.

"Well, honey it *is* a ship full of men."

"Do you know one of those dirty muggles made a pass at me? The one with the eye patch?" she said with her arms folded across her chest.

"He touched you?" Gangus asked, glaring at her.

"No. He became quite the gentlemen once I told him I was your wife. But I still don't like the way he gazes at me—like a drooling cyclops."

"Honey, you're still attractive. The years have not yet caught up with you." He smiled.

"I tell you I'm terrified, and you stand there smiling?"

"Sweetheart, I didn't mean to make light of your fears. If you wish, I'll

21

speak to the captain." He turned to leave.

"That is not really why I called for you."

He turned back. "Then why?"

She tipped past him and peeked out the door, making sure no one overheard her. Satisfied, she closed the door and turned to him. "When some men drink too much wine, they reveal much of what they should not."

"What have you heard, my sweet?"

"Celio got one drunk and had him talk about their real mission. He bragged that, after dropping us off, they would attack a king's ship full of treasure. Honey, these people are thieves…cutthroats. We may be in danger."

"Where are your jewels?"

"There," she said, pointing to a place where she'd hid them.

He pulled her to him. "There is honor among many Volarian men. I looked into captain Orroh's eyes, and he has assured me safe passage to Skatts Island. He gave me a note of introduction to give to a tavern owner who owes him a favor." He put his finger under her chin and lifted her head. Her beautiful brown eyes flashed up at him. "I will let nothing harm you," he assured her.

"You trust him, then?"

"I trust no one with the people I love. If he has lied, Celio and the others know what to do. Captain Orroh does not know that I have fighting men on board."

"But, our weapons are still packed away."

"Celio and Dinary have been quite busy bees. They discovered a locked cabin full of them."

A grin stretched across her beautiful face. "The gods bless you, my husband."

"I promise you, no matter what happens, we are all getting off this ship in one piece. Now, lock the door and open to no one but Dinary and me."

She nodded. Gangus kissed her gently on the lips. When he left the cabin, he heard the latch click as he walked off to find Dinary.

After dinner, the women gathered in Brehira's cabin to brush each other's hair and complain about the dingy bed sheets and food. The men had gone to the large cabin at the end of the ship. It was the largest cabin and where the captain had meetings with his crew. Tonight, it was used for drinking and singing and, of course, strange adventure tales from each of the men.

Hours later, the women went back to their cabins as did the captain and some of the men—minus the ones running the ship and those at the top of the sails keeping watch. The night was quiet.

*****

Days went by, and everyone began to feel more comfortable and trusting of one another. The women cleaned the cabins, washed the bedding, made the cabins quite livable, and to everyone's delight, they took over the cooking. The nude portrait of the dark princess disappeared from the wall. Gangus wasn't surprised.

The women complained to their husbands about the long journey. They were tired of washing and wearing the same clothes. Brehira assured them, just one more week and they would reach Skatts Island where fresh clothes, clean water, and good food awaited them.

In Dinary's cabin, Celio sat swilling wine. He brought the jug down and wiped his mouth with the back of his hand. "I heard one mate speak of a treasure map hidden on board," he told Dinary.

Dinary chuckled. "Every captain or shipmate has a tale about a treasure map. It's as old as the gods. There hasn't been a real treasure map for centuries."

"Hm…I'd like to think there is," Celio said, guzzling the rest of the wine.

*****

In one of the servant's cabin, Rhia stood braiding her sister Lucia's hair. "A few more days and nights and Skatts Island will be ours," she said excitedly "I can't wait for my feet to touch land," Lucia said. The sisters talked about hot baths and washing the dust from their hair—and finding husbands.

As everyone settled back and reflected on what they wanted to do once they landed, something hit the ship with such force, the lanterns turned over, and a small fire flashed up from the floor. Nearly everyone was thrown against something. Pieces of the ceiling fell, injuring some men. Women were screaming and calling for their husbands. The captain's men practically mowed Gangus' men over, running in the same direction.

"Oh, no. This can't be happening again," Celio shouted.

"What did we hit this time?" Dinary asked.

"The ship is under attack, you fools!" said one of Orr's men. "Either get out of the way or help us," he said while running up the stairs with a sword in his hand.

The ship had been rammed, and the mates from the enemy ship had jumped onto Orr's ship, and a battle had begun.

"Great gods!" Dinary said. He yelled to Methius to gather the women—put them in one cabin and for him not to leave them alone. He told Celio to hand him the weapon he was holding and for him to get more to pass out to his men.

"I'll go and find my father," he yelled over the loud shouts and thundering noises from above.

As Dinary was on his way down the hall, a mate from the enemy ship jumped from the staircase and stood in front of him. He appeared young, about twenty, with his head wrapped in cloth like a gypsy. He advanced on Dinary with his sword raised. Dinary's sword clanked against his several times, then Dinary, being a master swordsman, did a circling maneuver with his sword and lifted the man's sword from his hand. It went flying up in the air. Dinary lunged forward running the man through.

"Um, that was short work," he said to himself.

He heard footsteps behind him and suddenly turned into a fighting stance. He relaxed when he saw it was Gangus running up on him.

"Father, we're under attack! Why have you left Mother?"

"She's safe in the cabin."

"You stay with her! I'll join our men on deck."

"But this is not our fight, son!"

"We can't take the captain's generosity and not help him in his hour of need!"

"All right, then! Let me go see to your mother! And I'll join you!"

"Then you'll need this." Dinary handed Gangus his sword then brushed by him, scooped up the dead man's sword and ran up the staircase to join the battle.

Gangus ran back to his cabin, shielding himself from the falling debris, he braced himself for a sure fight with Brehira once he told her he and Dinary would help the captain whom she loathed. He opened the door and found her lying on the floor. The ramming of the ship had knocked her unconscious. Gangus saw that she was still breathing. He lifted her onto the cot and covered her with a blanket. He thought it was good that at least she wouldn't know what was happening. He locked the door and ran to the staircase.

But half way up, an enemy's foot landed on his chest and sent him hurtling down the stairs. Gangus fell backward. When his head connected to the floor, everything went black. The enemy stood over him with his sword and raised it. An entire blade of a sword came out of the man's abdomen as Celio ran him through from behind.

When Gangus came around, Brehira was putting another cool cloth on his forehead, and one of the other women was pressing a cup with a nasty-tasting liquid to his lips. He parted his lips and swallowed, then tightened the muscles in his face.

"That is awful," he said, still grimacing.

"Stay quiet. You've been out for days."

"But the fight....what..."

"We won the fight, Father," Dinary said from across the room. "That is, the captain and his men did. We helped a little," he said, turning to Celio.

"And the enemy ship that attacked us?"

"We set it on fire. It's probably still burning in Ebus," Celio said smirking.

"I'm proud of you, my son...you too, Celio. Wish I could have been there."

"Yes, you missed the whole thing. You sure you didn't fake being out? I mean, Father all you had to say was that you didn't want to fight. But to throw yourself down the stairs..." he teased.

"Ha ha," Gangus uttered rolling his eyes at Dinary.

"You leave your father alone. Here," Brehira pushed a basin to him, "go fetch me more water for your father's wounds." Dinary grabbed the basin, still grinning, and left the room.

"You know what the good news is?" Brehira asked, "We'll be in Skatts Island in two days. The ship wreck and ship attack—all behind us. If I never see another ship or ocean for a while, it will be fine with me. Promise me we can stay at least a month or so before boarding another?" she said, her eyes pleading.

"All right. I've had enough as well."

The days flew by, and not too soon for Brehira and the women. They pulled into Port Raven at Skatts Island days behind schedule due to the damages to the ship. The little town was called Orange Tree. Captain Orroh would have to lay over to get the ship back into shape. Gangus thanked the captain for his hospitality; the captain thanked him for the use of his men.

"Your men fight quite well to be just farmers. You never mentioned they had other skills. " Orroh said with a slight smirk.

"There were many things I failed to mention, and for good reasons, I thought at the time."

Orroh laughed loudly, and then his smile became genuine. "I like you, Lord Abram. You're like me. Trust no one." He extended his hand and Gangus pretended to shake it, but instead, he placed a small emerald in the captain's palm. The captain gasped and smiled then the men parted. Though both swore they would someday cross paths, Gangus secretly hoped he'd never see Orroh again. He liked the captain, but Orroh had far too many enemies for Gangus to be a friend.

Being in a strange town, Gangus didn't want to reveal Brehira's entire jewelry collection. With the note Captain Orroh had given him, he went to the tavern to see the owner. Sure enough, the man knew Orroh and was very helpful to Gangus in directing him to the right people. "Just tell them Tedor sent you," the tavern owner said.

The first place Gangus went was to a jeweler who specialized in rare pieces. Gangus handed him a two Karat diamond ring with two emeralds on either side.

"Exquisite," Mr. Pennypod said, examining the piece carefully. He didn't hesitate to place several pieces of silver on the counter.

Gangus frowned. "But I paid nearly two dragons if not more."

"I'm sorry, but that's all I have right now. But if you can wait a few days, I'm certain I can get you a buyer."

Gangus turned to Brehira. "Just take the money," she whispered. "We are all dying for a hot bath, some food, and a decent place to lay our heads."

He turned back to Mr. Pennypod. "All right, we have a deal." Gangus took the coins and placed them in his money pouch. Next on Tedor's list was the name of the landlord. Gangus needed to rent several cottages—all furnished. Brehira and the women went shopping for food and clothes for themselves and the men. After a few hours, everyone settled in for the evening.

Brehira hummed a little tune as she bathed and washed her hair in scented water. Gangus had bathed earlier and was sitting at a small table with pad and feather pen in hand. The servants sang as they prepared lamb chops with boiled potatoes, carrots, and green beans. A fruit pie sat cooling on the window ledge, and a jug of wine and freshly baked bread sat on the table.

The Chronicles of Bethica

Gangus wrote a notice he planned to have placed in every village in a couple of days. It read ADVENTURE: all expenses paid, one-way trip to a new world. Own the house you live in. Eat the foods you grow. Only men and women with skills are wanted. Sign-up sheet outside of Taylor shop. Be ready to travel in ninety days. Only leaving with the first seven hundred.

"Good," Gangus whispered to himself, examining what he wrote.

"Now, all you need is a ship," Brehira said, peeking over his shoulder.

Chapter Four

The Cristofur

Bang! Bang! The Chief Justice's wooden mallet struck the sound block that echoed throughout the long meeting room but was ignored by the nearly two hundred people pushing and fighting to sign up for the Paradise Adventure—a name that Brehira thought up at the last minute to add to the post. She said it would capture the imagination of the potentials.

"Get out of my way, you pompous fool!" a man shouted as he shoved a short bearded man to the floor and took his place in the line. Another scuffle broke out near the end of the line and then another in the middle of the floor. Cooler heads pulled them apart and continued to referee until they calmed.

"Citizens! Citizens!" the Justice pleaded. "If this unruliness continues, I will have all guilty parties removed and fined. Is that clear?"

Loud shouts of compliance rose from their lips in the stuffy, packed room. Outside, hundreds more waited. Each had a different story roaming in their heads. Many were simply poor; some were drifters and needed to belong; a few were bandits, looking to steal what they could—making the next port their 'getaway' route. But most had real dreams and hopes for a better life, willing to risk everything, even their lives, to make the journey. Many worked long hours trying to pay off a debt to crooked land owners who continued to tax their wages. Some were tired of farming other folk's land. Because of limited water supply, women spent most of the day carrying water from the wells. And many more were tired of the stench they had to endure from animal traffic which left the streets swarming with rodents and flies. There seemed little or no work for men; no real future for children, and a limited supply of husbands for young maidens. Men and women traveled from other nearby villages and small cities as well. The Paradise trip just had to be everything it boasted, some had said.

Unfortunately, being poor and having hopes and dreams wasn't the criteria for a seat. Settling in a new land required people of skill. There were Guilds needed. Guilds of Masons, and millers—of Black Smiths, and carpenters, bow and arrow makers, as well as other artisans. Needed also were midwives, physicians, scholars, priests, entertainers, expert swordsmen, farmers, fisherman, and the like.

As the sign-up sheet filled, the line from the outside moved quickly inside. There were less shoving and more polite chatter. It had taken some people days to travel from their villages to Orange Tree. By the end of the day, twenty-five hundred names were on the sheet. Only the best seven hundred and fifty would be chosen. Later that night, villagers and city dwellers who had signed up hoped that, in three weeks, their names would be among those who had made the list. People who had never prayed before, prayed that night.

*****

Captain Dulcy P. Dordrecht, a red-bearded man with green eyes in his mid-fifties, was Gangus' fifth interviewee. Dinary had been sent out to spy on each captain's claim of having the ideal ship. Dordrecht captained The Cristofur, a former war ship that had endured many wars. Brehira worried that it had seen its better days. But workers rebuilt it into a three-story passenger ship with small individual chambers for the captain, upper staff members, and Nobles. It contained a lower chamber for storing ropes and sails; also, it slept the officer in charge of the prow who had a staff of his own that stayed only in that chamber and carried out whatever was needed. Another chamber held the compass reader who also watched the stars and winds and pointed out the routes across the sea. On the same level was where the weapons were kept, and next to them, a berth that house the ones who would use them.

Then there was the great spacious middle chamber for the passengers. It received no light except for what came through the four hatchways. In the hold, everyone would have their own berth or space. Because of its width, between the berths was where the passengers would keep their chest and trunks and other private property.

The lowest chamber housed the kitchen which was not covered, and beside the kitchen was the stable for the animals that were to be slaughtered; sheep, goats, calves, oxen, cows, and pigs all would stand there together.

Gangus and Brehira walked with the captain out of the dining area and into the sitting room.

"That was a scrumptious meal, Lady Abram. At sea, I don't get many well-cooked dishes."

"I hope this is only one of many, Captain," Brehira said. She left the men to talk and went into the next room. Gangus and the captain sat facing one another.

"So, Captain," Gangus said, "What makes you so eager to join my suicide journey?" Both Gangus and the captain chuckled because that was exactly what the critics of the project were calling it.

"The notion started when I was a young man. I was going to have my ship and explore the ends of the world. Also, like most young men at that time, I let a pretty little thing change my mind. I loved her. Her name was Lititia. I bought a little farm, we married, and she gave birth to our son, but he soon died. A year later, she gave me a beautiful daughter, but the Black Fever took them both. I was devastated. I sold the farm. Bought a little ship and kept working my way up to bigger ships." The captain sat back in the chair.

"That's a lot for a man to handle. At least you were able to fulfill your dream of traveling."

"That's what I thought until I read your post."

"Ah…you're looking for danger," Gangus said smiling.

The captain leaned forward with a little boy gleam in his eyes. "Lord Abram, what you're proposing is exactly what I want. A trip to the unknown. I don't know if it's truth or fiction about this Endless Ocean. Men have returned so shaken up and vowing never to go again. Some never returned. Tales say they found paradise and stayed; others say monsters ate them."

"And you are willing to risk your men and your ship?"

"It's what I've always wanted." The captain grinned sheepishly and sat back. "Listen to me. Here I am going on and on about why I want to go. What made you decide to undertake such a project?"

"My reasons are rather complicated. I don't really know how to explain it. Perhaps someday when we're out at sea."

"Out at sea?" The captain's back straightened. "Did you say…out at sea?" His face brightened. "My good Lord Abram, does this mean you've chosen me?"

"You have what I need," Gangus said with a smile. "Sixty ton, three-story former war ship, seventy-four feet by two hundred and eighty feet, two hundred and fifty crew members, able to support over seven hundred passengers and carry a years supply of food and other goods, proved itself in many battles of war, and still appears to be going strong." Gangus leaned forward with his hand extended and said, "Welcome to suicide journey."

Captain Dordrecht grinned and almost shook Gangus' hand off. Gangus and the captain celebrated their new partnership with silver goblets of the

31

Abrams' finest wine. Afterward, The captain rose to leave.

"I better be heading back," Dordrecht said, "so I can tell my men the good news and get things started. Prepare the ship and give her a good once over."

"The ship is still in fine order, I gather?" Gangus asked rising from his chair.

"Oh, yes. It just needs to be shined up a bit."

He walked the captain to the door and opened it. "Safe travel, my good captain…until we meet again."

"Thank you, Lord Abram," he said. After getting into his awaiting carriage, he waved as the driver pulled off.

That night, Brehira sat up in bed laboring over a list of things to pack, while Gangus lay next to her pretending to be asleep but worried if he was about to take over seven hundred people to their deaths. Down the hall, the servants talked of enjoying as much time as possible on land since they would be spending many, months at sea. In the next cottage, Dinary fingered the eagle necklace on his chest, realizing he might never see his brother again.

*****

The trees were already filled with red birds on the expected day on the list. It was daybreak and the orange sun still faintly gleamed over the stone buildings, animal pens, and fields. The stray dogs and cats stretched and took their separate walks behind the butcher shop. A pig had already been gutted and the innards put in a slop bucket ready to be discarded out the back door. It seemed their breakfast was but a butcher's throw away.

For weeks, Brehira had meticulously checked the backgrounds of every candidate. The skill levels of those who had won a seat were extremely high. There were many people with the same skills, so if one or two were ill or got sick and died, there would be others to take their places. The list was expected to be posted throughout Skatts Island around noon. Because expectations and tempers were high, the Chief Justice had asked the king to send soldiers to discourage any rioting that might occur.

At Port Benet, The Cristofur glittered under the morning sunlight. The ship was tan and dark green trimmed in gold. Its square-rigged masts sat high above the deck like a crown. Hundreds of workers had been hired to sweep, scrub, and polish cabins, halls, and decks of the ship. It was one of the better-built ships of its day. People composed songs about its use in great battles.

The Chronicles of Bethica

If it completed its next journey, songs and poems would hail it as the greatest ship of its time.

A little past dawn, soldiers landed on Skatts Island. They made their presence known by riding up and down the streets and into the various villages. They walked in and out of shops, helping themselves to whatever they wanted: apples, pastries, a leg of lamb, a baked chicken. No one dared to speak against them. These were minor soldiers not paid as well as those who defended the king's interests in far away lands. Even their uniforms were not as fine; it bore the same colors, but many were second-hand–worn and faded with sloppy patch work. But they still possessed the authority of the king. So, opposing them was not wise.

Before noon, the streets became crowded. It was good for business as the owners continued to run out of food and drink in their now standing-room-only shops. A few minor fights broke out, but soldiers who showed little patience with such behavior quickly crushed them.

Well past the noon day sun, people grew intolerant when the list bearer failed to show up at noon as promised. They discovered later that the bearer was detained in a nearby town when a group of men pulled him off his horse and took some of the scrolls from him. When they didn't see their names, they beat him. The bearer jumped on his horse and fled for his life.

As time ticked on, people got restless, and tempers flared. In Crows Tavern, someone slapped a woman, and two men who injured each other in a knife fight got arrested. Greatly past the middle of the day, the list bearer's horse trotted into Orange Tree. Word of his coming spread like a grass fire. People stumbled drunk out of taverns and poured out of shops. The street and sidewalks were packed as the street buzzed loudly with conversation. The bearer slowly got off his horse. Fighting his way through the crowd was useless until the soldiers muscled him in with no problem. As the list went up, the crowd grew silent. The list was huge, and the writing was small. The man was escorted back to his horse; he mounted and trotted to the next town.

One by one cheers, laughter, tears, and anger marked the mood at each viewing. There were no riots just anger and cursing and disappointment on the faces of many who didn't make the list. Those who did rejoiced with tears and uncontrollable laughter. Many celebrated in the streets with singing and dancing. The shops closed. People went home, and the streets were soon empty. Only the soldiers and street cleaners remained. Gangus' post had caused quite a stir. There hadn't been that much excitement in Orange Tree since farmer Rodsaff's temperamental bull got loose and terrorized town folk and villagers for two hours before an arrow pierced his heart. To this day, Lord Abram's Paradise Journey continues to be the most talked about event in the history of Skatts Island.

*****

The day had arrived. The Cristofur had docked and was being loaded; seven hundred and fifty people had assembled to board. The Abram clan was finally leaving Skatts Island. Orange Tree had been their home for nearly five months—longer than anticipated. Dinary sat silently looking out the coach window. The servants, Celio and the men occupied the other carriages that were behind. Everyone seemed excited but had talked about not truly being prepared for the long journey.

"I'm going to kind of miss this place with its slow pace and quietness," Gangus said.

Brehira frowned. "Of course *you* would, you're a man."

"What does that have to do with anything?" he asked.

"Do you know how many trips me and the servants had to make to the well? Who do you think provided you with fresh water every day, the gods?"

They passed by many people who lined the streets to wave at those who were heading to the port. Some too poor to afford a horse or a mule had set out walking at dawn. In the carriage, however, the ride was only twenty minutes.

The carriage pulled in front of the port. Gangus saw loved ones who hadn't made the list kissing and wishing family members as well as neighbors a grateful farewell. Many town people and villagers just showed up to signify and get a glimpse of the famous Cristofur. The crew members greeted Gangus and Brehira and unloaded their trunks from the horse-drawn carts.

Though the ship was huge on the outside, nothing prepared them for the comfort and splendor of the cabins. The inside of the ship was very spacious. Everything that one could need or want was among the supplies of the ship. The crew was well groomed and polite.

"Honey, you made a great choice of the captain and this ship. The cabins are lovely. It's better equipped than the village we just came from." Brehira kissed him on the cheek and went back to their cabin to unpack.

"Lord Abram," Captain Dordrecht called out.

"If we're going to be spending several months together, I think it's time you call me Gangus." He then turned and said, "And this is my son, Dinary."

"Happy to make your acquaintance, Dinary. Welcome aboard."

"Thank you, sir," Dinary said nodding to the captain. He then turned his focus to Gangus. "Father, I think I'll go down and start unpacking."

"All right, son."

"Well, Gangus, why don't you go on down and get settled as well. We'll be pulling out presently."

"Good idea," he said. He left the captain and headed for his cabin. It was the second largest—the captains' being the first. Everyone seemed pleased with their accommodations. In the early morning sun, the Cristofur pulled out of Port Benet, never to darken its port again and headed for the journey that had been ordained by the gods through the Oracle Naman.

Chapter Five

Stowaway Princess

"How does it look, Kofius?" Captain Dordrecht asked his Sail Master.

"The wind is not blowing abaft the beam, sir. We have to tack our sails on an eighty-degree angle to the wind."

"Won't that slow us down?"

"Aye captain, about two knots, sir. But we'll make up that time once the wind is more favorable."

"Good. I'll be on lower deck two if you need me," Dordrecht said.

"Aye, Captain."

As the captain left Kofius to his duties and descended the stairs, he noticed Judian, the Quarter Master, patting his foot to the sounds of the Cornamuse, crumhorns, and lute that rose from lower deck one. Judian was second in command of the ship. He was a bright young man in his thirties who had left home at fourteen to find adventure upon the seas. When he returned to his little village five years later, he found that most of his childhood friends, their relatives, and his entire family were dead from the plague. He listened to the steady beat of the tabor drum that nearly matched the rhythm of his heart. The melodic vibrations lifted the darkness from his spirit.

The festive music was a delightful resonance to the captain's ears. As he entered the gathering, he looked over the crowd and spotted Gangus in the middle of the floor with Dinary, Celio, and several other men dancing to a hundred-year-old tribal dance of their Volarian ancestors. Brehira led the women in circling the men and clapping in time. The men had wide smiles as they high stepped and kicked to the rhythm of the lute.

While Dordrecht stood mesmerized by the music and dancing, a magician in a multi-colored costume stepped up to him. He removed the captain's hat— tapped it three times with a wand, and a dozen birds flew up into the ceiling then disappeared. The captain laughed as the magician skipped away. When he placed his hat back upon his head, he made a face as if his hat didn't quite fit. When he pulled it off again, the entertainers pointed and laughed as Dordrecht reached up and discovered a bird's egg on his head. Another magician danced up and took the egg out of the captain's hand, placed the egg in his own mouth, then pulled his own earlobe and the egg appeared to fall out of his ear. The magician laughed and danced away. Every entertainer wore bright multi-colored costumes with funny hats to match. There were also jugglers, singers, dancers, and strong men; the women stood around and felt the muscles in their arms. As Dordrecht was caught up in the activities around him, one of the men grabbed him and pulled him into the circle of dancing men, and the Captain began to high step and kicked with the best of them.

As Dinary kicked and turned, a young maiden caught his eye. He was staring so hard that he bumped shoulders with Celio. She had dark brown hair, soft white skin, and the bluest eyes he'd ever seen. She was dressed the way most maidens dressed for special engagements, white, long sleeve tunic with an emerald and gold overdress. He watched her walk out on the deck.

"You're going to stand there with your thumb up your nose? Go talk to her," Celio shouted over the music while dancing.

Dinary was embarrassed that his actions were so obvious. He looked around to see if anyone else had noticed. Then he slowly squeezed between those who were dancing, singing and playing instruments—careful not to bring too much attention to himself as he followed the maiden who had caught his eye. When he reached the deck, he found her looking up at the stars. Dinary stood a distance from her pretending to be enjoying the night air but admiring her from the corner of his eye. She turned to him suddenly with a smile that made his heart skip a beat.

"Your father steps well for a man of his age," she said.

"Every male of my tribe is taught that dance at the age of four."

"Then that accounts for the perfection in the performance. I really enjoyed it."

"What about your Father? I bet *he* dances well."

She looked away from him as if he'd insulted her. When he saw her reaction, he told her he was sorry if he'd said something wrong. She told him not to apologize and that she was an only child and her parents were dead. He apologized again. Then after a few moments, he formally introduced himself, and she told him her name was Myrah.

"That's a beautiful name."

"Thank you."

Dinary, feeling shy and not knowing what else to say to her, made his apologies and left Myrah on deck looking up at the stars. Later that night, he felt foolish that he'd acted like a little boy.

Days later, Dinary ran into Myrah again. She was coming from her cabin and him from the supply room. They spoke briefly and went on their way. Weeks went by, and many had noticed them spending quite a lot of time together. Celio once walked up on them while they were kissing; they broke apart when Celio deliberately cleared his throat. Dinary had forgotten that he was to help Celio with the inventory of the supplies.

"Oh, thank you, Celio, for introducing me to the woman of my dreams," Celio teased.

"Thank you for what? I introduced myself. You had nothing to do with it."

"Like the gods I didn't. If it weren't for me, you'd be still standing in the middle of the dance floor staring at her with your mouth gaped open and your thumb up your nose."

"Why do you keep saying thumb up my nose?"

"That means you were looking like a mindless little boy."

"I was not."

"Yeah, thumb up your nose," he teased grinning. The two continued to bicker at one another all the way down the long hall and into the supply room.

It was obvious that Gangus adored Myrah, and Brehira was already planning the perfect wedding though Dinary had not yet asked for his lady's hand. But after weeks of courtship, Dinary finally led Myrah out on deck one night under the stars—where they had first introduced themselves—and presented her with his grandmother's sapphire ring as a token of his lifelong love and devotion. She gladly accepted it, and the two kissed to seal their bond. Then Dinary called a gathering, which was their custom, and presented Myrah as his bride-to-be. Cheers went up from the crowd, and she was ceremoniously accepted into the Abrams' family by an all-female traditional dance. All the males then danced to celebrate Dinary's position as her new husband and head of his own family.

The wedding took weeks of planning. Wedding garments had to be measured and sewn, and food prepared for over seven hundred people, including crew members. Everyone was excited about the wedding but talked of being mentally sea sick since they had not walked on land for weeks. There was no reason to dock as everything they needed was aboard. They just needed to get the sea taste out of their mouths, Gangus had said.

The plan was to be on land for three days, give the boat a thorough checking, buy new clothes and board for the remaining months at sea. Brehira wanted to buy silk thread for the wedding and ceremonial garments. The cooks remembered a special spice needed for the wedding meal that wasn't on board. They would buy some once the ship docked. Everyone was excited to see land. Dinary and Myrah were just happy to be together. And after all of his teasing, Celio found his lady among the musicians.

Her name was Detria, and she was a young widow of twenty-seven with no children. She said her father was a drunkard who beat her mother then abandoned the family. Her mother fell on hard times and had to sell Detria into bondage when she was only ten, just so her mother could feed her younger brothers and sisters. After being mistreated, Detria ran away and joined a minstrel group. There, she had met her husband who taught her to sing and play the lute. They married, but a year later, he died a soldier in a far-away land. Celio courted her for only a few weeks before he asked her to marry him and she accepted with glee.

There were so many weddings and engagement celebrations that Gangus had to put an even tighter limit on food and supplies if they were to survive the long journey. He also reminded them that there were only two more stops in the Volarian realm before heading towards The Endless Ocean. Gangus gave these reminders by way of several posters on each deck. The people were disappointed but understood.

*****

Early one morning, Captain Dordrecht was alerted by the stress signal that came directly to his cabin. This was done so no one would hear news before the captain heard it. It kept the rest of the crew from panicking. "Great Zuse, let it be a false alarm," he said to himself as he raced to the upper deck. The crew members frowned and mumbled among themselves when they saw the captain running. "How does it look, Kofius?" Dordrecht asked.

"It may not be anything, Captain. But I've been watching that ship," Kofius said, nodding at a ship that trailed behind, "and it's been tailing us for quite a while."

Dordrecht put the optic to his eye. "Did you do the test?"

"Aye, Captain. Every time I speeded up, it speeded up. When I pretended to get off course, it went off course."

"Good job, Kofius," the captain said while he watched the ship through the optic. "Sound the alarm," he said, taking the optic down from his eye. "I'll be on the War Deck."

"Aye, Captain."

Gangus, who was dressing and readying himself for the morning, heard the alarm then feet thundering overhead like a herd of horses. "Merciful gods," he said out loud. The captain sent word informing Gangus so he could prepare his men. After hearing what the messenger had said, Brehira rushed to Gangus' side. He hurried her out to join the other women in an appointed place and ordered soldiers to guard them. Then he joined with Dinary, Celio, and the rest of the men on the War Deck to get instructions from the captain. But, in the midst of the instructions, a crew member came with a message that the ship in question was a royal vessel sent by King Zular. And that no one was in danger; they just needed to speak to the captain.

"Who is this King Zular?" Dinary asked the captain.

"I've heard of him. But what could he possibly want with me?" Dordrecht said while brushing passed the men and heading for the stairs.

"What do you want us to do, Captain?" Celio asked.

"Do nothing until you hear the alarm. Then come running with everything you've got."

Captain Dordrecht reached the upper deck where Judian introduced him to General Brutus.

"General Brutus, you needed to speak to me?"

"Yes. I am here in the name of the king. King Zular's daughter, Princess Lerayah, was kidnapped. She's been missing for over a year. We thought her dead. Then the Shanghai of the king's daughter reached him by a messenger. And we have orders from the king to stop any vessel in these waters and search it." The general handed Dordrecht a scroll of his authority to search.

"There is no one on this ship by that name. And...you have no jurisdiction in these waters.

"If you would open the scroll," the general said nodding towards it, "you'll see the names of every king in this area lending their command in helping to fine King Zular's daughter."

Captain Dordrecht unfolded the scroll and, sure enough, there were the royal seals of the twelve kings. He sighed. "He's right."

"This is an insult," Judian scolded. "We are not pirates. For you to think we would be involved with doing such a thing is not just an insult but absurd."

"It's all right, Judian. I'm sure the general means nothing personal. He's just following orders. Besides, the quicker they search, the quicker we can be on our way."

"Thank you for your understanding and cooperation, Captain." The general signaled with a hand gesture for his men to come aboard and search the ship. He led several dozen well-armed soldiers to every part of the ship, starting at the top. Judian and Dordrecht accompanied the general on every detail. When General Brutus reached the main birth, Gangus, Dinary, Celio, and the rest of the men stood with hands on their swords and a stern look on their faces.

When the general saw their body language, he gestured to his men to halt. "Your captain can vouch for us. We mean you no harm. We have orders to search this entire ship. We are looking for Princess Lerayah."

"The king's daughter was kidnapped and dragged onto a ship," Dordrecht said. "They have the authority and my permission to search."

After listening to the captain, General Brutus again signaled his men to advance but was startled to hear metal slide against metal as the Abram clan half drew their swords when Brutus and his men took a step forward.

General Brutus frowned. "But didn't you hear what your captain said?"

"No disrespect to our captain," Dinary said, with his hand still on the handle of his sword, "but our women are back there, and no one is going near them."

"There's no woman by that name on this ship, anyway," Celio said.

Brutus raised his voice. "We have our orders." He took a step, and Dinary drew his sword as did his men, and General Brutus drew his sword as did *his* men.

Suddenly, Captain Dordrecht jumped forward. "No, No. Wait! Please." He looked pleadingly at Gangus. "Just bring the women out and let them see she's not among them and they will go. Please, Gangus, Dinary, please. Think of your women."

Gangus agreed and ordered Celio to bring the women out.

"But, Father!"

"Let them see she's not here, son so they can leave. We've wasted enough time."

Celio walked down to the end of the hall into a large room they used for celebrations. He came out ahead of the women and kept them several feet away from Brutus and his men.

Brutus strained his eyes. "I can't see from there."

Celio spoke loudly, "This is as close as you're going to get."

Brutus called out to the princess, but none of the women answered him.

"This is ridiculous," said one of Brutus' captains. And he made a motion, but Brutus threw his arm in front of him. "I'm tired of this game," Brutus said. "I'm going to count to three, and if your men don't stand down, blood will flow. One...two..."

"Don't!" a woman yelled. She kept her head and face covered, then moved towards Brutus and his men. "I'm Princess Lerayah," and she removed the covering from her head and face.

When Brutus and the king's soldiers saw the princess, they immediately bowed before her.

Dinary's eyes grew wide. "Myrah!"

"I hope you realize this means death to everyone on this godforsaken ship,'" Brutus said waving his sword.

"But, we didn't know who she was. She lied to us!" Judian shouted.

"How could you deceive my son and put this whole ship in danger?" Brehira scolded. "Take her!"

"Lord and Lady Abram, Dinary. Please let me explain."

"I think you'd better," Dinary said, glaring at her.

Princes Lerayah walked forward and stood directly in front of General Brutus and his soldiers. "No one kidnapped me. I, with the help of some very kind peasants, put that story out so my father would think me dead and stop looking for me."

"But why, Princess?" Brutus asked.

"You know why. My father is not a good king. He sends his soldiers to conquer, pillage, and enslave poor innocent people, raping and stealing their lands. He's over taxed our people until they are starving to death."

"But, Princess, once you're queen, you can make right the things you think are wrong."

"You don't understand. The people hate my father and the entire royal family. By the time I'm queen, there will be no country to govern. I'm not going back with you."

"Then, blood will flow, Princess. I know how you feel. But my loyalty is to your father."

"Then let the blood flow," Dinary said with his sword in a striking position. "My future wife is not going anywhere with you."

Princess Lerayah's face brightened, and she looked over at Dinary and smiled.

The men on both sides stood in a fighting stance with swords drawn. Suddenly, Brehira very calmly asked General Brutus to talk to her privately. He told her there was nothing to talk about—and that nothing she could say would make any difference—and if she wanted to help, she should try to talk some sense into her husband and his men. Finally, after much insistence by Brehira, General Brutus gave in and walked with her into her cabin. Gangus and Dinary were opposed.

When they walked into her cabin, Brehira offered him wine, which he refused. He voiced his annoyance when she kept insisting that he lie to the King about the whereabouts of the Princess. General Brutus became very disagreeable and turned to leave.

"General." He turned back and stared coldly at her. She told him it was rude for him not to accept her hospitality. He sighed then picked up the cup and drank until he nearly choked on one of three large gems she had placed in the goblet. "You can build yourself a castle, have the pick of women from the best families, no more killing—no more taking orders from kings or anyone else, ever," she said.

"You really believe I'd betray my king for gems? You don't know me. I'd never do that."

"I kind of figured you weren't the type to accept that kind of offer. So, here's another—I'm going to tear my clothes off and scream. Now I know most of your men will leave here alive and some of ours may die. But once that door opens, fifty men are going to rush in and cut you to pieces before your soldiers can get to you. What I'm saying, General, is whatever happens, you're not leaving this room alive. Now, is that worth taking a woman back to where she doesn't want to be…only to have her run away again? If she did it once, she'll do it again."

Brutus stared at her without blinking. He looked at the door then back at her. "If there's anything I can't stand is a woman who thinks she's smart." He scooped up the gems from the cup, placed them under his top garment and left the room. The general walked briskly past the Abram clan and told his men they were leaving.

"But, what about the princess?" one of Brutus' soldiers asked.

"What princess? Let's go," Brutus commanded.

"But…general…"

"Go, I said!" Brutus and his men marched up the stairs followed by Judian and the captain.

When it was certain that the royal ship had gone and the women were safe, all focused their attention to Brehira who stood in the doorway of her cabin.

"Honey, how by the gods did you get him to change his mind?"

Brehira thought for a moment and then said. "I guess it was something in the wine. The blend *has* been in your family for generations." She turned and closed the door behind her.

Gangus looked at Dinary and Celio dumbfounded. "Did she say wine?"

Chapter Six

Never-ending Ocean

Gangus climbed into bed as Brehira sat on the edge of it combing her long, dark hair. "All right," he said. "We're alone now. How did you get the general to change his mind? And don't give me that, 'something in the wine' talk."

She looked over her shoulder at him momentarily, but didn't say anything and continued combing. He sat patiently waiting for her to respond when she finally lay the comb aside and slid into bed next to him.

"Well?" he prompted.

She gathered the covers around her and pulled them up to her waist. "I offered him gems, but he refused them. So I told him I'd tear my garments and scream if he didn't abandon his mission to take Myrah. I mean, Princess Lerayah."

"But, we would have killed an innocent man. It's not like you, my sweet, to lie."

"Innocent? She didn't want to go. And you heard him. He said blood would flow. I had to do something."

"But, Brehira...lie?"

"I wasn't going to risk losing the people I love," she said, raising her voice slightly. "I did what I had to. We live in a harsh world, and only the gods know what more lies in store for us out here at sea."

"Honey, I'm not accusing you of anything. I'm just sorry that a woman as righteous as you had to be put in such a position. I don't want this journey turning any of us away from our Volarian upbringing. Maybe this trip is a mistake."

"Don't you dare talk so. I trust that the gods spoke to you. Everyone is excited about this journey. I've heard no one speak harshly of it. Now, get some sleep, you're worrying over nothing." She leaned in and kissed him then settled back and closed her eyes. Gangus frowned. He blew out the light and slid down under the covers. He thought—*Dear gods, I pray she is right.*

The next day, there was bad news. Port Whymore and Port Somesner were the only two ports left in the Volarian realm before heading to the Endless

Ocean. Now there was only one, Port Somesner. The closest port had to be bypassed due to a bad fire that burned most of the supply shops, killed farm animals and scared off small game.

After pulling into the port, Gangus and Brehira decided to stay behind while Dinary, Celio, and the other passengers readied themselves to leave the ship.

"Snap to it, you lazy swine!" Kladius yelled at two new shipmates he found idle at their stations. "See to the anchors," he growled. Kladius was the ship's boatswain and was responsible for the crew, including training young, new crew members, and for preparing and looking after the ship when it docked. He was a good man, and the crew members liked him, but he could be tough on trainees.

By midday, Dinary and the others had returned to the ship, and the first lower deck was loaded with new goods, tools, dry foods, and livestock. When the ship pulled back out to sea, everyone was excited about the journey and the new land Gangus had promised them.

By late evening, Dinary decided to take a walk with Princess Lerayah on deck out into the moonlight. They stopped and looked over the edge at the sparkling waves. Dinary loved the way the moon lit the shine of her brown hair. She turned to him, and he gathered her into his arms and passionately kissed her. After the kiss, she rested her head on his chest, and he kept his arms around her.

"Are you excited about our wedding day?" she asked him.

"Very."

"Whenever I bring it up, you don't seem to be."

"I'm sorry," he said. "I have a lot of important things on my mind."

She lifted her head and smiled up at him. "And what could you have on your mind that is more important than me?"

He looked down at her. "There is nothing more important than you. It's—just my father."

"What—is he ill?"

"No. Nothing like that. He's worried. He pretends he's not. But I know him. Worrying about the people he asked to accompany him on this journey is wearing him down. I can see it on his face when he thinks no one's watching."

"My stars, I didn't know," she said.

"Yes, that's why…Ahh!" Dinary yelled out in pain then staggered back from her. His face was wrinkled tightly, and he was holding his chest.

"Dinary!" Princess Lerayah yelled frantically. She pulled his hand from his chest, and her eyes grew wide.

"What is it?" he asked looking down. The necklace was glowing, and the sapphire had turned ruby red. He frantically grabbed the chain of the necklace, yanked it over his head, and tossed it over the side of the ship. They watched as the waves gobbled it up. The princess looked back at Dinary's chest and gasped. The entire print of the necklace had burned into his skin. Then, slowly, as they both watched, healthy, olive flesh emerged over the scar.

They looked puzzlingly at one another.

"What in the name of the gods *was* that thing?" she asked.

Dinary, still looking like he'd seen a ghost, answered, "It…it was a gift from my brother. B…but it's never done *that* before."

"Did your brother tell you where he got it?"

"No. He had worn it since we were children."

"Perhaps your father would know."

"I don't think so. He would have mentioned something. Besides, Father has enough on his mind. I'm not going to bother him with this mystery." He looked down at his skin, "I wish I knew why that necklace did that."

She looked out at sea. "We *are* entering strange waters," she said above a whisper.

"Please don't mention this to anyone. Not until I understand it myself," he said.

She turned her face back to him and smiled. "I won't. It'll be our little secret."

"Thank you." Dinary held her around the waist as the two of them walked back inside.

"At least I don't have to worry about your wearing that thing on our wedding night," she said.

Feeling some relief after being spooked by the necklace, he welcomed her humor. Throwing his head back and chuckling loudly, he said, "That makes two of us."

After Dinary had walked Princess Lerayah back to her chamber, he noticed Gangus with that same troublesome look on his face, making his way up the stairs.

"Is everything well, Father?"

"Yes, I'm just taking this map up to Rhicer."

"I'll check in on Mother."

"She's asleep, but you can still check if you'd like."

Rhicer was an old Sea Artist—the best of his kind. He was not only an expert compass reader, but he could read the stars and winds and could point out any route at sea. He could guess the coming weather just by how the waves struck against a piece of wood or other floating objects in the water. When Gangus entered his chamber, Rhicer was busy reading a chart and turned to greet Gangus. "Well, Lord Abram, you're up pretty late. Couldn't sleep either, hey?"

"No. I could. I just wanted to see what you thought of this. It's rather strange. The Oracle gave it to me." Gangus handed him the map.

Rhicer glared at Gangus as if he were looking at a crazy man. He took the map, unfolded it, and turned it sideways up. After taking a few moments to examine it, his mouth fell open. "Merciful gods, man. Did you say an Oracle gave you this?"

"Yes."

"I've met lots of characters who, in my day, pretended to be Oracles, which is why most people laugh when someone says they spoke to one. I almost laughed at *you*. But I believe you did get this from an Oracle of the gods. You must be someone very special. Do you understand it?"

"Hardly, that's why I brought it to you."

"It's a star map...not just *any* star map. Some believe the gods created it themselves. Only a few of these exist in the world. It can take you through any waters, no matter how far, dangerous, or mystical. You can't get lost if you know how to read the formation of the stars. I know of only three men in our realm who can read these—I'm proud to say I am one of them."

For the first time, Gangus could breathe freely. "Rhicer, I can't tell you what a weight you've just lifted from my chest having said that. Because now I know for sure that the gods indeed blessed this journey."

Gangus sat up most of the night—fascinated by listening to Rhicer explaining the different formations of the stars and what they meant.

Down below, Dinary slept deeply. In the dark silence of the room, a spot lit up on his throat and the necklace re-appeared around his neck. It lay against his skin, still and cold; the glow from the sapphire eye broke through the blackness of the room. The eye blinked, and its wings moved as the eagle slowly turned its head and looked up at Dinary. The other side of its face was blank. Dinary, still asleep, shifted over on his side—the necklace dangled and rested against his hand. The sudden heat from the metal woke him. When he saw the necklace, he jumped. Dinary lay in the dark clutching it and wondering about its mystery. Strangely, he smiled. It was all he had that belonged to his brother.

Meanwhile—on the top deck, Kofius signaled the captain. He narrowed his eyes as if he couldn't believe what he saw. Under the bright beam of the moon sat a battered ship with dark, torn sails—each torn piece flapping in the night wind. Shadows appeared to dance across the deck of the abandoned ship as it slowly rocked to and fro against the toss of the waves. The prow was ten feet above the bow and was carved into a huge winged creature that looked as if it had come straight from the pits of Hades. And in each of its skeletal hands were real swords that were three times the length and width of any humanoid-made blade Kofius had ever seen.

Captain Dordrecht rushed in. "How does it look, Kofius?"

"Captain, I think you need to see this."

Chapter Seven

Ghost Ship

Kofius steadied The Cristofur as it drew near to the abandoned ship. The ships were side-by-side and, Captain Dordrecht peered through the optic but saw no movement—no sign of life. The ship was a Veddenn warship used by high-class traders and sailors over several hundred years ago. The captain lowered the optic and frowned. "That's odd," he said to Kofius. "Why would a ship that old still be at sea? And who left it there?"

"That's exactly what I was thinking. Old worn out ships like that are usually found broken apart and lying on the ocean floor," Kofius said.

"Take her to six."

"Aye, Captain." Kofius increased the speed, pushing the multi-ton vessel past five knots and leaving the abandoned ship well behind.

Captain Dordrecht hid the fact that, during the trip, he had become quite nervous about this paradise journey. He'd told Rhicer that, while he was excited about the journey, he felt it might be anything but paradise. One reason was that ships hardly ever sailed out of the sight of land. Navigation relied on landmarks, tides, nature, and other indicators to safely reach their destinations. The captain regularly checked with Kofius on the course while the helmsman steered according to Rhicer's instructions. There was no land in sight which made this paradise journey questionable for Dordrecht. Needing to converse with Rhicer, Dordrecht attempted to return to the middle deck when Kofius blurted, "That same ship, Captain. It's...it's up ahead!"

"What do you mean, up ahead? It can't be the same ship."

"But it is, Captain. I recognize it."

"That's impossible. We left it at least a league behind," Dordrecht said while swiftly putting the optic up to his eye. Then he snatched it down. "Holy gods of the sea. I...I don't understand."

It *was* the abandoned warship that Kofius and the captain saw. And they continued to see it several times that night. They would speed past it, only to spot it up ahead minutes later. Kofius even went off course a few times, trying to lose it, but each time, they would pass it again and again. Captain Dordrecht didn't want to alarm the others until they could figure out what to do. They thought they had when the Cristofur was brought back on course and, for nearly an hour into sailing, the ghost ship had, somehow, disappeared. For hours, the captain used his optic searching for any trace of it but saw nothing.

At one point, Dordrecht laughed nervously and said that perhaps he and Kofius suffered the same mirage. But they both knew it was no mirage. And that nonsensical notion came abruptly to an end when the ghost ship rammed them from behind, sending the captain and Kofius flying across the deck.

The jolt woke up the entire ship, throwing people into the walls and sides of the ship.

"Man overboard!" a shipmate blasted. The helmsman was knocked over the side. But before his shipmates could reach him, the ship was hit with another thunderous thud and several others who had tried to rescue the helmsman also tumbled over the side. This caused further rescue efforts to be abandoned, and the men were left in the water where they were struck and killed by the attacking ship.

Kofius was hurt badly, and Captain Dordrecht lay unconscious. As second in command, Judian managed to reach the first deck and took over the ship. "Lead the women to the safe chamber!" Judian yelled down to the lower decks. Soldiers, not knowing what was happening, grabbed swords and scrambled up to the first deck with them drawn, but soon fell over like injured ducks in a pawn when the Cristofur was rammed yet again with such force that their swords flew out of their hands. Some were badly injured by their own swords when they tumbled head over heels down the staircase.

Gangus and Celio also came running to the first deck. The alarm was sounding. There was yelling and running. Archers scrambled to get to their war stations and were ready with arrows drawn. Then the mysterious ship moved along side of them, and the men couldn't believe their eyes. The ship that had no one aboard now had an entire army of skeleton soldiers attired in war gear that dated back several hundred years. At Judian's command, the archers shot their arrows; each arrow met its mark, but there was no flesh or vital organs to be hit. The archers and commander stood in awe as the arrows flew through empty eye sockets and nasal openings—nicking the bones of their cheeks and piercing their heads and necks with no effect. The skeletal army jumped from their ship to the Cristofur, and the battle began.

The women in the lower decks prayed to the gods to help their men. The thundering footsteps they heard from above were nerve-racking. They could hear the shouts and battle cries. Above the first deck, as the swords were striking and sparkling under the moonlight, lightning cracked the sky and thunder roared. The heavy rain put the men at a disadvantage. It was as if the gods were on the side of the Dead Ones. The men were so outnumbered and engrossed in the battle that no one noticed when three of the skeletons slipped by them and made their way to the lower decks. As they descended the stairs, not one bone of their feet touched wood. They floated down a hallway, then turned completely around when they heard chanting coming from the other end of the hall where the women were praying. They continued following what probably sounded to them like babble. They turned a corner and soldiers in charge of guarding the women immediately confronted them. A fight pursued, but the three ghost warriors made little work of mortal flesh.

The women were kneeling—calling on the gods and getting their attention when the door flew off its hinges and sailed across the room. The women's screams pierced the ceiling and nearly shattered the glass in the chamber lanterns. High pitched screams rose steadily as the undead soldiers floated towards them and lifted their swords. Some of the women continued calling on the gods with their eyes closed, or dropped, as if dead, to the floor. Brehira, thinking this was it for them all, feared for her husband and Dinary and hated the thought of never seeing her eldest son again. *If I can take just one with me,* she thought. She picked up a lantern and threw it at one of the demons; it caught fire, but this sudden ball of flame, undeterred, turned its attention fully on Brehira. She, feeling the heat of the flames as they floated toward her, threw up one hand to block the blow and covered her face with the other as the skeletons raised their swords above her head. Suddenly, her hands felt warm and glowed. She snatched her hand back and stared at it. When she saw that the demons were terrified of it, she lifted her hand, not quite knowing what to expect—but hoping the gods had done something. Right before her very eyes, the demons fell into a heap of gray ashes and their swords disappeared in a flash of light. The women, not sure what had just happened, crawled over to Brehira—whimpering and lay at her feet for protection. Brehira just stared off, confused and speechless.

On the top deck, Celio was being fought hard by the things with no eye balls, but it still seemed to see him. Just as it was about to strike a deadly blow, Celio ducked then came up and cut off the skeleton's sword hand, then its head, sending it over the side of the ship. Celio turned to see who to fight next when he spotted Gangus in trouble with two skeletons on him. He ran to Gangus' side and, together, they took down several of them, cutting off their heads and arms which sent them thudding to the floor of the deck in pieces. Both turned and saw that Judian was down. He had been stabbed in the shoulder and lay on his back still fighting with his sword while the blood gushed from him, and the skeleton stood over him and battled Judian relentlessly. It stabbed Judian again but had its head whacked off by Gangus, and then its torso cut in half by Celio. Gangus and Celio looked around to see who to help next and what they saw were numerous skeletal bones and their heroic shipmates standing, dripping in their own blood with their swords at their sides. Then a loud cheer went up. Gangus and Celio helped Judian off the floor. The men ignored their wounds and greeted one another with wide smiles and bearhugs of victory.

But that victory wouldn't last. Slowly, every head turned toward the ghost ship; a loud cracking sound like wood breaking rose in the night air. The men stood with their mouths gaped opened and their eyes wide as the carved creature opened its demonic mouth and sucked air into its wooden body. The loud cracking of the wood when it turned its head towards the men sent chills up Gangus' spine. The eyes were the only things not made of wood. They were flesh, black and bulging; they had a sinister gaze, like those of a fallen Angel. The loud cracking continued as the statue wrested itself from the bow. It was a giant, nearly twelve feet tall and broad as an Ogre, dressed in a red garment down to its wooden feet with tight sleeves and a hood covering its carved head. Its facial expression was placid as its demonic eyes bore a gaze that chilled the humanoid soul, and in both its ligneous hands were huge giant-size swords. Its wings shot out with a sound like a strong wind blowing. Its wings were six feet wide on either side and, as the wings flapped, it made both ships rock from side to side. The demon flew over onto he Cristofur and hovered for a moment. Then it flapped its wings until it rested its feet on the floor of the deck with a loud thud that unsteadied the balance of the ship. The demon stood looking down on the men with both swords out to its side—its giant wings tucked and folded inward as it took a battle stance. Another roar of thunder cracked the sky.

The men stood together and braced themselves. They were practically blinded by the heavy rainfall as they stood there and bravely prepared themselves for whatever the outcome. The archers shot their bow—aiming for the eyes, but the demon batted each arrow away. Several ran up to it and stabbed it, but there was no blood, just splinters. Then they all ran up to it, cutting it, trying to find its vulnerability—and shooting arrows one after another. The creature fought back, swinging its mighty swords back and forth, cutting men in two, and sending several heads into the ocean. The soldiers fought hard for several minutes but to no avail. They never even made a dent into hurting it. The fallen men's blood covered the floor boards. The ones who were still standing stood back from it—banding together for strength in numbers and ready to launch another attack.

"Maybe we can set it on fire!" someone yelled.

"No, we'll burn the ship down," Judian managed to say; he was still bleeding from his wound. Gangus and Celio were on either side of Judian holding him up.

"But we're no match for it. I'd rather burn and go down with the ship!" another yelled.

"But think of the women!" another answered him.

Just then, Dinary, as if he'd been kept asleep until this crucial moment, stepped through the crowd. He wasn't afraid, and he looked the demon in its black, lifeless eyes. The statue stumbled back when it saw the necklace. Its entire focus seemed to now be on Dinary. The men watched but couldn't understand the moment. Dinary carried two swords, something he'd never done before. He stood in a fighting stance and waited for the creature to make its move. Several men bravely walked up and stood next to him, but Dinary told them to go back.

"Are you mad?" Celio yelled to him.

Dinary never answered, but remained focused on the demon. It was as though he was awake but in some trance. Suddenly, the creature raised its massive sword and brought it down upon Dinary. But Dinary brought both swords up, blocked, and held it up with the strength of a giant. The men gasped at Dinary like he was some new and improved being.

Then, Dinary leaped to the side of the creature, took both his swords and severed one of the creature's hands. The huge sword thundered to the deck floor, and Dinary tossed the hand and picked up the sword like it was a feather.

"How the stars did he do that?" asked Judian. "That sword weighs more than a man."

The men stood amazed as Dinary sliced and cut away at the creature, but never received one cut from its mighty sword. The creature became frustrated and gnashed its wooden teeth together because it knew it would never defeat him as long as he wore that necklace. The creature tried many times to sever Dinary's head and free him from the necklace, but Dinary's body movements were as swift as a mouse dodging a hungry predator.

Gangus couldn't take his eyes off Dinary. He couldn't believe what he was seeing. Dinary's movements were gallant and smooth. The massive swords clanked and glittered as the rain beat upon them. The creature swung and missed at every turn, but Dinary connected his blade with ease, cutting off wooden chunks of it—whittling its legs until they split and broke in half. The demon went down to the floor. A great cheer went up from the men, and Dinary swooped in and rammed the massive blade into the eye of the creature. Blood gushed out like a small waterfall. Then it burst into flames that turned into a whirl wind and disappeared. The ghost ship also burst into flames and, as the men stood frozen, it formed into what it always was—a demon from the pits of Hades, burning and growling—with fire and red bubbles all around it. It let out a thunderous roar like several mighty lions and then sank. The fire danced upon the water for a few seconds before the ocean swallowed it.

First, the men stood quietly and stared. Then loud cheers broke the silence; the men grabbed Dinary and held him up on their shoulders. Gangus blew out a breath of relief as Celio and Judian looked at each other speechlessly. While the men continued to celebrate Dinary and their victory, Captain Dordrecht, Kofius, and Judian were finally taken down to the physician, while Kladius and Rhicer took over the sailing of the ship.

As Gangus and Celio made their way to the stairs, they passed their shipmates who were picking up the skeletal fragments of the demon soldiers and throwing them over the sides of the ship. The rain helped in cleaning up the blood-drenched deck. Laughter and talk of Dinary's heroic fight were heard throughout the ship.

Victory, however, would be bitter sweet as, days later, they would have to prepare the Ocean burials of those who didn't survive.

Chapter Eight

The Island of Gorr

Brehira stood on deck watching Dinary staring out over the blue waves. The early morning sun shined brightly and made the beams that were peculiar and strong turn the ocean's white foam to a pale golden hue. The warmth of the wind touched the faces of all who embraced the sunlight. It shined hot as blood ran cold concerning the unknown all were about to encounter.

Dinary, so enthralled with his thoughts, didn't hear Brehira walk up to him. He jumped when she gently touched his shoulder.

"Mother," he said quickly, turning his head towards her.

"I heard ravings of your brave stand against that horrible creature," she said. "I wish I had seen you."

"I wish I had seen me, too," he shot back.

She giggled. "What do you mean?"

"Mother," he said, not looking at her, but as if he were talking to all that surrounded him. "It was as though I was in a trance. I don't know where my strength came from." Then he gazed into her eyes. "I shouldn't have beaten that thing."

"It's these waters, son. This is indeed a strange ocean." She purposely neglected to mention her own dark and strange victory against the skeletal creatures that resulted in her saving the lives of herself and the women. She had made the women swear to secrecy. "The answer you seek must be in Bethica. Otherwise, the gods would not have led us here," she assured him.

Dinary smiled and held her shoulders. "I believe you're right, Mother. Like Father, I've always loved the beauty of your wisdom."

*****

It had been months since the ghost ship battle. And several more since the Cristofur had set sail from Skatts Island. The travel had been quiet and uneventful. Then slowly, gentle neighbors who had been kind and thoughtful suddenly turned vicious when food and water became scarce. The lack of food and water brought on madness. People fought over scraps of food, rags soaked

59

with water and herbs for loved-ones who suffered from various sicknesses.

Brehira prayed until her hands brightened and began to tingle. It was then that she discovered her ability to heal. Just a touch of her finger turned water into wine. Beasts of burden had to be killed for meat. But soon, even after stretching the rations, food source quickly diminished.

Morality was down, and there seemed to be no divine intervention for that. But Gangus, greatly respected, managed to bring the people back to their senses. But not before breaking up numerous fights, some even ending in murder. He went into his chamber and fell to his knees. "Oh, Raziel...wise and all-knowing god, you promised me kingdoms in a paradise land, but all I have is a ship full of mad, starving people. What have I done to displease you? I don't know what to do. Help me. Please!"

As Gangus lay prostrate on the floor, the fog rose above the Ocean. It was a wet, thick mist that had a taste—not salty, but gritty, like sand. The Cristofur cruised under the speed limit—about three knots; the fog lifted, and faint orange clouds began to disintegrate into odd shaped pieces across the sky. Shiny patches of bright yellow that skipped upon the greenish waves made it clear that they were no longer in Volarian waters.

A bell rang out frantically signaling land. Gangus rose to his feet. He lifted his eyes to the ceiling. "Oh Lord...my god, thank you."

In the far distance, a long brown strip—flat, some hilly and several giant masses rose high upon the surface. Multiple months had passed since Gangus' encounter with the Oracle. As hours passed, the Cristofur, moving ever closer, revealed a dark soil-covered land with hills and the tallest mountains ever seen by Volarians.

Two fifty-feet beige stone pillows on either side gated the entrance to the shore line. The stones were carved into creatures with no genitals and one large eye in the middle of their faces just above the mouth. They had no noses, but upon their heads were a single horn shaped like a dagger.

Everyone aboard stood or sat silently as the ship passed through the gate, mindful of just months before, a wooden statue had come to life. The swordsmen and archers were ready for battle—never taking their eyes off of it. Only after cruising a distance from it, did all breathe a sigh of relief, but quite unaware that the fleshy eyes of the stone creatures came alive and followed their every move—magically recording and reporting the ship's whereabouts to those who waited on land.

The Chronicles of Bethica

A small party began to leave the ship including, Captain Dordrecht, Celio, swordsmen, archers, and the dark-skinned Volarian, Olutunji, who served as their Striker—an expert hunter, big fish fisherman, with knowledge of medicinal plants and herbs. Because of his great strength, he too served as a warrior. With his six foot spear, he could knock a bird right out of mid-air as it flew hundreds of feet in the sky.

Gangus brushed past Dinary. "No, Father, you should stay. The people are still unstable, and they will only listen to you."

Gangus raised his hand—a gesture to silence him. "If this is the land," he said, "then I should be the one to investigate it. The people respect you as my son. They will listen to you as well."

Dinary, though not pleased, nodded in agreement.

Hungry and weak from a lack of food, Gangus, and the men left the ship.

The land from a distance looked uninhabited, but as the party ventured on, they discovered a strange flock of red creatures flying overhead and even stranger ones—green with sharp dagger-like beaks that sat upon thick branches on leafless trees. The men were so hungry, one spoke of plucking one out of the sky with his arrow and cooking it right on the spot. But the creatures appeared dangerous; Gangus thought finding creatures not so resistant would be better considering his weak and feeble body.

The ground consisted of dark orange dirt and scattered gray and black stones which made the pathway rugged. As they rounded a curve on the path, there, stood a fifty-foot wall made of unpainted wood with a large oval entrance way. Three large skeletal heads hung above the entrance.

Suddenly, there was a scream, and one of the archers fell over with, what looked like, a large ax in his back. Gangus looked down and thought he recognized the weapon. TROLLS! He yelled.

Celio, protecting his Lord, shoved Gangus behind him. The rest of the men quickly surrounded Gangus like a Volarian wall.

"What the devil are you doing?" Gangus said angrily, looking around the circle.

"You cannot die," Celio said with such seriousness that it took Gangus aback.

"The people followed you here," Celio continued. "And you must not die. Just stay between us, and if we fall, you head back to the ship."

"But—" Gangus managed to say.

"Here they come!" Celio interrupted with a shout. "Holy Father of gods. They are not trolls and look at the size of them. Archers! FIRE!"

The eight Ogres stood ten feet high and nearly the same in width. They appeared humanoid—though their round, bloated, wart covered bodies defeated that notion. Like serpents, they could dislocate their jaws to swallow huge chunks of prey. But weak as the men were, they gathered strength from the depths of their souls, for they were not about to become an Ogre's banquet.

As Celio's shout rose above the archers' heads, the arrows penetrated Ogre's skin like tiny needles that did nothing to slow the creatures' charge. Each creature carried a large stone meat cleaver covered in dried body fluids. With one swing, the remaining archers dropped as their heads flew like a blur past Gangus' eyes. Celio lunged at one. The Ogres' eyes widened as the steel blade; something Ogres had never felt, easily sliced through its throat. Never having seen a blade cut so easily through Ogre flesh, the remaining Ogres seemed reluctant as they stood with ugly blank faces. Gangus saw his chance and broke through the flesh wall that was holding him back. He swung at a creature, but feebly. Unknown to everyone, Gangus had given up half his rations for weeks which had taken much of his strength.

Straight away, an Ogre grabbed Gangus' sword arm and raised its cleaver, but just as the blade came down, Olutunji's spear pierced the creature's neck, and just as quickly, another Ogre knocked Olutunji to the ground. Celio ran over to Gangus and helped him to his feet. As they both looked around, they noticed Olutunji lying still on the ground not far from his other fallen comrades. Only Gangus, the captain, a few men, and Celio were left.

"Go," Gangus shouted to Celio.

"Forget it! I am not leaving you, My Lord. We fight together. We die together. Now, stay behind me, and I will finish this, they are just smelly old Ogres after all," Celio said smiling. And Celio's white teeth were the last things Gangus saw before all went black.

"Gangus …. Gangus," said a voice from the darkness. "Wake up," the voice said again. Gangus opened his eyes, and there was Celio's face all bloodied staring at him.

"What happened? Where are we?" Gangus asked, frowning.

"Sir, I'm sorry. I really thought I had them." Celio dropped his head. "They were just too strong."

"And too well fed." Gangus shot back in a tease. "Think how well we would have fought had we eaten a leg of lamb before we got here." Gangus, always the father-figure and still fuzzy in the head about his whereabouts, tried to ease Celio's disappointment with himself.

Celio chuckled half-heartedly.

"It's okay, son. We're still alive. What about the others?"

"I'm afraid it's just me, you, Captain Dordrecht, sir and a few men."

"And Olutunji?"

"He didn't make it."

Gangus grew sad hearing that as his eyes had adjusted to the darkness. Shadows became clear visions, and he finally realized they were caged in what appeared to be a deep cave. "So, we're prisoners," Gangus muttered.

"More like dinner," said a strange voice.

"Dinner...who said that?" Gangus demanded. "Show yourself."

Out of the darkness, glowing blue eyes, like twinkling stars moved ever so obediently towards him. Behind the almond shaped eyes was a feeble looking humanoid dressed in what used to be an elaborate robe, but now faded and worn. Its skin was as white as alabaster, and on each side of its head hung long pointy ears that leaned away from its face.

Gangus could see that the creature was sickly and many years his junior and he greeted the old humanoid in kind. "I am Lord Gangus Abram."

"I am Lord El' Tendar," he said with a slight cough. "Though it is hard to tell," he looked down at his tattered clothing, "that I was once Lord of any-thing." He paused. "I notice you speak Domarian. I've never before seen *men* of your race."

"If we share that language, believe me, it is quite coincidental. For, we are Volarian from a land far away" Then Gangus said, "Just how long have you been here?"

"I no longer count the years. I'm from the Qu'Venar race and fear those who loved me have forgotten me by now."

"You said something about us being dinner."

"Oh, no not me. I'm too useful to these beasts. You see, they like to be entertained. I'm forced to perform my arcane arts for the chieftain. First I re-fused, but they'd tortured others in front of me...giving me a taste of what I'd get. So I took the coward way out. I'm—so ashamed."

63

"Nonsense. We all do what we can to stay alive," Gangus assured him.

"Arcane arts?" Celio asked, appearing clueless.

Lord El'Tendar chuckled softly then coughed. "I gather there's no magic where you're from?" he asked.

Gangus told him since they had entered this realm, that magic didn't seem all that strange to them anymore. He didn't tell him of Brehira's many abilities because he wanted to make sure El' Tendar was someone he could trust.

"Why don't you use your arts to escape?" Celio asked.

I'm much too weak to muster up that kind of spell anymore."

Celio lowered his head. He felt sorry for the old guy.

*****

Olutunji felt something nibbling his hair, and then a sniffing sound, followed by a deep growl. He flashed open his eyes and stared into the yellow twin irises of a wolf-like creature. It was massive and from the shoulders—as tall as a young bull. The creature bore its sharp fangs that dripped saliva onto Olutunji's forehead. He knew why the beast hadn't eaten him. Being an expert hunter, he knew of herbs to rub into his skin that made his flesh undesirable to carnivorous animals. But Olutunji still had to think fast, because the herb may stop him from being eaten but not from being torn to shreds. He had learned a technique taught to him by his grandfather, who also was a great hunter of his tribe. Slowly rising from the ground, Olutunji narrowed his eyes to a thin slit and kept them peeled to the creature's eyes. He held his gaze, without a single blink, and stared into its soul until the creature became quite spooked and began to back up slowly. After a few minutes, the creature tucked in its tail, turned, and pranced back into the wooded area from whence it came. Olutunji then blew out a breath of relief and flopped down to the ground. Sweat poured from his brow as he laid his head against the bark of a tree. "Whew! Thanks, grandfather," he mumbled to himself. Then he thought about Lord Abram and the men. *Were they devoured or carried off by the Ogres? I must find out.*

He put his tracking skills to use and followed deep footprints that appeared to have been made by humanoids and Ogres. The footprints led him to the Ogres' camp and far away from where he had been knocked unconscious and left for dead among his deceased comrades.

The Chronicles of Bethica

After scouting the area for hours, he observed Ogres taking what he perceived to be prisoners to an entrance within the camp. Stealthily making his way to the entrance, he came to a staircase leading downward. He quietly walked down the spiraling stone steps into a dark place that reeked of stench. As he settled at the end of the stairs, he called out to Gangus. He called out several more times and was startled when he finally got a response.

"Help us!" a voice answered back.

"Sounds like Lord Abram," he thought out loud. Then he heard several cries for help. He continued to follow the cries, hoping it wasn't a trap. The stench thickened in his nostrils and he began to gag. As Olutunji continued to follow the cries, his heart raced when he passed by numerous body parts of different creatures in countless barrels. Some barrels were for heads only and some for eyes, feet, tongues, and hands.

There were also lots of cages with different kinds of creatures in them. As Olutunji passed the cages, the creatures reached their hand between the bars and begged, in their strange languages, to be let free. But his only concern was for his comrades.

Some of the caged creatures were without hands, feet, and eyes. Some made pitiful noises through their painful stares into space.

"Holy Father of gods. What have you guys stumbled into?" Olutunji whispered. "And where the Hades are you?"

"Here!" he heard Lord Abram and several of the others cry out frantically.

Olutunji's eyes brightened when he saw his Lord and comrades. The cages were made of wood, and Olutunji hacked away at the bars with his sword. Then, with all of his strength, he pulled the whittled wood apart with his bare hands until they splintered and broke. After Gangus had been released, he and Olutunji released Celio, Captain Dordrecht, and what was left of Gangus' men.

"Let's get out of here," Olutunji said, leading the way up the stairs.

"Wait! I want you to release my new friend. He's back there," Gangus said, pointing to Lord El' Tendar's cage.

Olutunji didn't hesitate but went back and hacked away at the cage and broke in. They were surprised when the old Lord didn't rise. Gangus told him, "you're free, come with us." But he gestured with his finger for Gangus to come close. He told Gangus about a magic staff that was taken from him when he was first captured. He said the Chieftain kept it near the altar. He pointed out to Gangus a flat stone tablet with instructions and the command words written in his dried blood that he had hidden under the straw that had been his bed for years. Gangus pulled the stone from under the straw and begged the old one to come with them. It was then that he revealed to Lord El'Tendar Brehira's healing gifts.

"There is no way her powers can reach me here, and I'm too old and weak to travel. If you should ever meet my people, don't tell them of my miserable existence. Tell them I died in the luxury of my arcane gifts." And then he said in a weaker voice, "Promise me."

"I promise," Gangus told him.

With that, Gangus rose and led the men passed the cages of hands reaching for them and pleadings in languages unknown to them when, suddenly, they heard a female voice say, "You idiots are not going to leave us here?"

Gangus and Olutunji looked down upon their feet and below, looking up through an iron grate in the floor was a pair of blue eyes staring up at them. It was a female, and she instructed them on how to get her and her sister out. Gangus found two iron bars that were sharp at one end. He handed one to Olutunji, and they pried up the grate, pulling the young females free. They were beautiful and tall, like amazons, and were partially nude. The men gave up some of their clothing. The older female threw her golden hair out of her eyes as she covered her nakedness.

"It's a good thing we decided not to leave," Olutunji said smiling.

"What do you want—a trophy? Let's get out of here," the oldest sister said. Then, she looked around for where the Ogres kept their weapons and spotted a locked door. With her great strength, she kicked it in.

Olutunji was taken aback. "Great god, she's strong," he said.

"And ungrateful," Gangus replied.

There, she saw various weapons leaning against the wall, on tables and lined side by side on the floor. She and her sister began to toss weapons aside until they gazed upon their own: a six-foot spear and matching decorated shields. She handed the sword to her younger sister. Gangus and the men found their weapons also.

The sisters hurried toward the door. The older sister turned and snapped, "You want us to leave you behind, or are you coming?" She didn't wait for a response. She and her sister peeked out then ran off.

"Leave *us* behind?" Gangus said. He and Olutunji exchanged puzzling glances then took off behind the women.

When they finally caught up to the sisters, Gangus took over the lead. He put the stone tablet into a medium size pouch and handed it to Celio. "No matter what happens, don't lose this," Gangus said sternly. Celio took the pouch and nodded.

As he, his men, and the Domarian sisters inched closer to where the Ogres were gathered, he could hear deep laughter from the Ogres and cries from their victims. Ogres love to play games with their prey. They would order them to run around then set out to catch and batter them before devouring them. Hiding back in the thick of a group of bushes, Gangus couldn't take the game any longer. These weren't their men; he didn't even recognize the little creatures, but his heart went out to them. With large cleavers, a few Ogres were chopping off limbs and eating them while the creatures screamed and squirmed. Then Gangus noticed the Chieftain, and next to him at the altar, Lord El' Tendar's magic staff.

"Well, what are you waiting for," the older Domarian sister muttered. "Are you going to kill them with your eyes? Aaaahhh!" Was her battle cry as she ran into the mix with her spear held high —her sister right on her heels. The younger sister hit an Ogre right between the eyes with her blade her older sister sliced open the belly of another, spilling his guts onto the ground. Gangus and Olutunji looked at each other and hunched their shoulders then ran out and teamed up on an Ogre, slicing into him and severing his head. The chieftain rose from his thrown, grabbed a cleaver, and joined the fight. He was huge—over ten feet tall and just as wide. He swung a giant size cleaver that decapitated several of Gangus' men before the Domarian sisters finally took him down in a hail of cuts, stabs, and a blade through the eye. Gangus made his way through the flabby cut flesh of the fighting Ogres and grabbed the staff. With the staff in one hand and his sword in the other, Gangus aided his men and the sisters as all slashed their way through a herd of smelly Ogres—leaving them dead or fatally injured in their wake.

"Eww," the younger sister said looking around at what was left of the Ogres. She watched one gag on dark yellow bile as he fell to the ground—his dead eyes staring up at her.

Thanks to the Domarian sisters, the battle with the Ogres was over as quickly as it had begun. Gangus and the others stood panting with blood dripping from their weapons and a vast spread of dead Ogres sprawled upon the ground. Gangus led his party, including the Domarian women, Ndornah, and younger sister Melitah, back to the ship. Later that night, he practiced the spells using the staff.

As Dinary and Celio watched Gangus practice with the staff, they discovered that the weapon possessed great functions. Dinary was anxious to examine it, but Gangus grew very protective of the staff and, after every practice, would lock it away in a small room.

The Domarians were grateful for being rescued and for the promise of being taken back to their land. They offered to help the Volarians to secure good land in Bethica where they could settle and flourish as a nation

After a few days on the ship, Ndornah told the Volarians the story of how their Domarian ancestors were brought to Domari over a century ago. She said the Domarians, at that time, were an evil race and mistreated their female population by sacrificing them to evil gods. When the goddess Dahlia got wind of this, she transported the women to Domari to worship only her; and to ensure that no Domarian women ever suffered such mistreatments again; she gifted them with special abilities, making them bigger, stronger, and as capable as men.

All sat—intrigued as the sisters revealed more of their story.

Chapter Nine

Consequences

The sky was already filled with stars when The Cristofur pulled out to sea. The Damarian women caused quite a stir as they followed Gangus and the returning party from Gorr. While the crew stared with mouths gaped open, the women were quite unimpressed with the crew's childish behavior. They viewed the men like they were animals in a cage. The Damarian women were tall, with long, shapely legs that went on forever. They were quite different from any women Volarian men had ever seen. Damarian women were muscular, with smooth olive skin, and voluptuous bodies. As Ndornah, the eldest, and Meletah, the youngest, strolled along the decks, making their way down the staircase, Meletah's eyes made a note of one particular soldier that she considered quite suitable for mating.

Ndornah was displeased with her gaze, and she leaned in and whispered in her ear. "Do not look upon these animals with such passion, my sister. They are but dog vomit beneath your heels."

Tired of her sister's interference with her mate choices, Meletah pouted and walked faster ahead, leaving Ndornah well behind. The sisters were taken into Brehira's chambers and introduced to the ship's women.

Ndornah and Meletah finally relaxed and saw they were among friends. All of the men left the chambers. The women enjoyed getting to know the sisters and how they came to be in Gorr. It seemed that Ndornah, among many of her skills, was a big game hunter, and Gorr was noted for its large and challenging creatures. It was the place where Dedroyles, the warrior class of the Domari, came to train and sharpen their warrior skills. Ndornah is a Pramyma; these are the ruling and priestess class of the Domari. She dreamt of being a Dedroyle and wanted to prove she was worthy of such a title. Ndornah, eager to help her sister make her mark among their people, brought Meletah on the hunt, hoping to improve her skills. Meletah made a great impression, but on their return to the ship, they, along with the other Domarians on the hunt, were captured. Pramyma and Dedroyles tasted no differently to their captors whose abdomens protruded after gorging on their flesh. Thanks to Olutunji and the others, the sisters escaped that fate for which they were extremely grateful.

Later that evening, Gangus was polishing the bulb of the staff when Dinary entered his chamber. "Wow!" Dinary said. "Can I hold it?" He asked with his eyes all wild like a little kid's.

"I'm afraid not, son. This staff holds great and dangerous powers; we have to be careful that it is not mishandled. I hope you understand."

"Of course," Dinary said, feeling a little disappointed.

Gangus placed the staff in the small room, locked it and they all headed for the dining area for the evening meal. Captain Dordrecht, who sat at the head of the table, lifted his cup to toast their new ship guests. Ndornah and Meletah were delighted to have been shown so much attention and kindness. But Dinary, though enjoying the company of the sisters, couldn't quite get his mind off the staff.

"Thank you so much for your kindness towards Meletah and me, but I've noticed," she looked down into Brehira's cup, "that my sister and I were not served the dark water."

Brehira hesitated and looked over at Gangus for help—which she didn't get. "Ndornah, this is not water, its wine made of aged fruit and is very potent. It will make you dizzy if you're not used to it. We," and she looked back over at Gangus, "thought it best not to serve you, since you weren't used to its effects."

"Dizzy? Dizzy how. I'd like to try it," Meletah said grinning.

"Perhaps you could take some back to your chambers," Brehira said. "It will help you sleep."

"Very well," Meletah said. "I haven't had a good night's sleep since those beasts captured us."

Brehira breathed a sigh of relief. The last thing they needed, she thought, was a couple of drunken voluptuous beauties on board with a bunch of horny sailors scheming to get at them. And from hearing how well the sisters fought their way out of Gorr, Brehira wasn't sure if she was protecting the women from the men or the men from the women.

After dinner, mostly everyone settled into their chambers. Dinary couldn't stop thinking about the staff. Gangus had gone into the Captain's chambers to discuss the best course for the ten-day journey to Domari. Brehira was in the guest chamber with the sisters making sure they were comfortable. Dinary, itching to get his hands on the staff convinced a reluctant Celio to be the lookout while he went into his father's chambers and got it from the room. All he wanted was to hold this wonder in his hands, he thought.

A nervous Celio paced back and forth in front of the door. He put his mouth close to the door. "Come on. What's taking you so long? I'm dying out here."

Dinary didn't answer because he was frantically searching for the key.

"Dinary!" Celio whispered loudly.

Dinary was so desperate to hold the staff that he didn't care what lie he had to tell his father if he were caught breaking the lock. He took out a dagger and, with his new strength, he was surprised how easily the locked popped when he jammed the dagger into it. He opened the door and there it was. Dinary picked it up and turned it over and over in his hand like it was a precious gift from the gods.

The stone tablet that lay in the corner of the room caught his eye, and he picked it up to read; but the instructions were in the old man's language, and only Gangus, could interpret it.

"Dinary!"

"I'm coming!"

Dinary took a bed covering and wrapped the staff in it. He opened the door, and he and Celio scooted up the back stairway to the far end of a deck that was seldom used. He unwrapped the staff and examined it again. He was mesmerized by it.

"Can I hold it?" Celio asked.

He handed it to Celio who smoothed his hands over it and gazed at it from top to bottom. "You think it will make wind for the sails?"

"I don't know," Dinary said taking the staff back.

"Think how fast we could go places. Even if there is no wind."

"Yeah. Now, what were those words again for the wind?"

Celio struggled to remember. "Oh…you point it and say, 'Drabeck.'"

Dinary hesitated and then looked at Celio who gestured for him to go ahead and do it. He pointed the staff at a sail. "Drabeck," he said. A gust of wind shot from the staff and hit the sail jolting the ship with such force that everything that wasn't nailed down and every living thing on the ship was violently hauled forward. Sleeping passengers were thrown out of their beds onto the floor. Crew members picking themselves off the deck were puzzled. Gangus and Captain Dordrecht lay in the corner of his chambers with a look of shock on their faces. Suddenly, the bell sounded.

"I better go up and see what's happened," Dordrecht said.

"I'll go with you."

Gangus and the captain reached the first deck.

"What the devil are you doing?" Dordrecht yelled to Kofius.

"Nothing, Captain. It just suddenly jerked forward. I didn't do a thing. Honest."

"But that's crazy. A ship can't jerk forward like that on its own."

At the back of the deck, Dinary and Celio got up off the floor.

"What in the god's name did you do?" Celio asked, rubbing a sore spot on his head

Dinary looked at the staff. "I did what you told me to do." Then he thought out loud, "Oh no. I'm going to have to tell my father what we've done—and…" He turned, and Celio was gone. "Celio! I won't forget this," Dinary yelled watching Celio scramble out of sight.

"Captain, I swear to you, I did nothing."

But Captain Dordrecht continued yelling at Kofius when Dinary stepped into the doorway with the staff in his hands.

"Don't yell at Kofius, Captain. It's my fault; I did this."

Heads turned, and Dinary stood with his head slightly bowed, looking pitifully up at his father.

"Dinary, what have you done? Give me that." Gangus said, taking the staff from him.

"I'm sorry, Captain Dordrecht," Dinary said. "I just thought we could use it to make our own wind. To get places faster even when there's no natural wind stirring." He thought his idea would take the fault and anger away from him, but it did nothing.

Gangus' face darkened when he looked at his son. "You can't use this to guide a ship, you fool. This is a weapon, not a plaything."

"Don't talk to me like I am a child."

"I am your father, and I'll talk to you as I please. Especially when you behave with the mind of a boy."

"But, Father…"

"Silence!" Gangus yelled. "I apologize for my son, Captain. He's never disobeyed me before. I don't know what got into him. Tell me what punishment to give him—to make up for his foolishness."

Dordrecht appeared puzzled and scratched his beard. "I… don't know."

Judian stood smiling. "I do," he said.

The next day, while several members of the crew pointed and laughed, Dinary tried to ignore them as he busied himself scrubbing the deck on his hands and knees. "You forgot a spot!" one of the crew members joked. Next to him was Celio steaming with anger. "You just *had* to mention my name."

Dinary grinned and turned his back to scrub a spot he'd missed.

"Oh, you think it's funny? Well grin at this," Celio said, lifting the scrub bucket and pouring the entire contents of dirty water over Dinary's head. The on-looking crew howled with laughter.

Chapter Ten

Gifts of the Gods

The five-day punishment was over, and Celio and Dinary had made up and laughed about the whole incident. Even Gangus and Captain Dordrecht forgave the men. "After all," Dordrecht had said, "no one got seriously hurt." Gangus put the staff where no one could find it and kept a post at his door to make sure no one snooped around in his room when he and Brehira were out.

There were only two more days left of the journey to Damari. Ndornah and Meletah drew close to Brehira. They admired her kindness and wisdom. They had asked that she go with them to meet their people and she agreed.

Late one night, as Celio slept soundly, he had a vision. It was more than a dream—like someone was in the chambers and he was experiencing this event. Celio saw himself dressed in a white vest-like garment, down to the knee; on his breast plate was the symbol of the gods; his arms and legs were covered in gray wool; he wore a metal plate from his knee to his ankle. He wore a metal face mask with slits for his eyes, nose, and mouth. He was down on one knee peering up through the slits at a god who sat upon his throne and handed Celio a shield of light, and a sword; the glitter of the metal was so bright it was near blinding.

Celio shot up in bed—panting and sweating profusely. This was the third time he'd had that same dream. He never told a soul. But the dream worried him.

*****

Pulling into Domari was a glorious day for everyone, especially Ndornah and Meletah. The Domarian race primarily lived on the island of Domari where the Goddess Dahlia ruled over all, and high priestess Diana called the Grand Matron, one of the first Domarians, ruled under her, in the land.

The men were instructed to stay aboard, and only Brehira was escorted off the ship. When passengers and crew members saw in the distance all of the statues of female warriors, they finally understood what sort of kingdom the sisters inhabited. And while some found it interesting, a small group of men resented being prevented from coming on land.

"Who do they think they are—not needing a man? Let's show them what men can do," a yellow-teeth sailor said grinning. And he, along with three other men, left the ship to swim and find an unguarded location of the island so they could sneak ashore.

Brehira was taken aback by all of the beauty of the kingdom. It proved that these women came from a very wealthy, civilized, and artistic cultured environment. There were mansions, and libraries, places of learning, great ships, buildings for religious teachings, and farm lands as far as one could see. They escorted Brehira into a great temple where women from all walks of life greeted her with a warm smile. She saw no men, though there had to be some, given all of the children that she saw in military training. The girls looked to be no older than five or six.

The women pointed out to Brehira each statue of their ancestors. When Brehira saw that they were all draped in priestly garments, she knew the sisters weren't just ordinary women, and she was right, when, finally, they reached the altar and found their mother, the Grand Matron Diana, on her knees praying.

When their mother saw them, she wept and ran to them. "Thank the goddess, my babies," she said throwing her arms around them both. "They said you were dead, but I prayed to the goddess, and she has answered my prayers." She examined them. "Are you all right. Were you hurt?" Then she called for the medicine women.

"No, mother, we are fine," Ndornah assured her. "Mother, there's someone we want you to meet."

The Grand Matron looked over at Brehira. "Come forward."

Brehira walked forward, and a guard placed her hand on Brehira's shoulder and gently pressed for her to bow. When she bowed, the Grand Matron told her to rise and come to her. Brehira stood before Grand Matron Diana.

"This is Brehira, mother. Her shipmates rescued us and she was very hospitable and kind to us. We want to reward her and her shipmates for their kindness."

"Of course. You will stay the night." Diana clapped her hands once, and a guard stepped forward and bowed. "Take her to our finest chamber and provide her with whatever she wants."

"Sama shi," the guard said—which meant 'as you wish' in the Damarian language.

Brehira was taken away and accommodated.

"There's another matter, mother. Her gesgea, the leader of the men who rescued us, wants safe passage to a good land where they can lay down their roots and live in peace. I told them I would bring it before the council. They didn't know all that was needed was your approval."

"Then I take it you didn't tell them who you were?"

"We weren't certain until well into the journey that they could be trusted with knowing priestly blood was aboard."

"You did wisely, my daughter. You can tell Brehira that her mate's request has been granted."

"Yes, mother."

*****

Childish giggles rang out from beyond the bushes where the trespassing sailors hid. The giggles rose over the white water fall as the young beauties sat in their bright, colorful garments and braided each other's hair.

"Bless the gods, if my eyes have ever seen anything more beautiful," said one of the sailors—saliva streaking the corners of his mouth.

"Oh, look at that one," another said.

"That one's for me," said the third sailor.

"I don't know. I don't like this. No men around and these women don't seem to have any fear," said the fourth man.

"Oh, stop being such a woman."

"You haven't heard? These women are not ordinary. They fight better than some men."

"Ah —stories to tell little girls like you at bedtime." He laughed. "I want a closer look at these beauties," the yellow-teeth one said. And he moved closer to where the maidens had gathered.

"No. No." the fourth one whispered. "Don't." He turned and ran. The others started after him.

"Ah, let him go," he said, his yellow smile beaming. They turned their attention back to the women and followed him through the brush. The men ducked down and waited like snakes ready to strike. One beauty was so unknowingly close that one of the men could have reached out and pinched her and almost did when she suddenly thought she saw a large animal in the bush and screamed. Her screams alerted the other young women as well as the guards who ran in the direction where the girls pointed. Several armed guards took off to find out exactly what had frightened the girls.

After several minutes, the men rested in the thick forest. "I think we lost them," one of the men exclaimed and he proceeded to undo the front of his garments to relieve himself. As he stood basking in the glory of an empty bladder with his eyes closed, a blade suddenly struck him below the waist. He felt a sharp pain, looked down, and discovered to his horror that his private part was missing. "Bloody Hell!" he bellowed, looking over at the guard with his blood on her blade. He fell to his knees in shock while the other men grabbed their swords.

Several guards appeared—some with swords and some with spears.

"You blasted wenches!" he said through his rotting clinched teeth.

But only one stepped forward with her sword raised while the others stood back with their spears and shields.

"You gotta be crazy," one of the other sailors said looking at just one woman facing them.

As all three swords swung at her, the men found that she was stronger than two men. While the men struggled and panted, she barely broke a sweat. Her movements were swift as she practically danced around each man, making small cuts on them and smiling.

"What the hell are you?" one asked.

She blurted, "Your executioner. Shut up and fight—if you call it that," she said laughing.

The three men advanced on her all at once again. She danced and slashed arms, faces, legs, and abdomens. The men were a bloody mess, and she didn't have a scratch on her.

The one she had injured below the waist yelled. "She's a demon, I tell you." He tried to crawl away.

"Oh, no you don't," she said, reaching down and lifting him with one hand. Then she slit his throat and tossed him aside like he was a doll made of cloth.

"And then there were two," said one of the guards who stood watching. The other guards laughed.

"You're…you're devils. You're not women," he said clenching his yellow teeth.

The two men fought hard—but this time, they weren't aiming at her body, but her inferior sword and they cut it to pieces. "Ha!" he said, his yellow smile gleaming. But his celebration was short lived when she kicked her long legs up and caught him under the chin nearly knocking him out. She reached and grabbed his sword. Tired of toying with them, she cut and slashed the other sailor to bits, then turned on the one still lying on the ground.

"Just get it over with," he growled.

She stood over him and drove the blade through his heart. He gasped and went limp.

When the guards reported to their captain, they didn't mention the men but said they had tracked a wayward Seawolf and killed it. It was a believable lie. Seawolves had often been spotted in that area. They were called Seawolves because of their ability to swim great distances underwater. These wolves possessed an extra lung which allowed them to hold their breaths for several minutes. They were the only wolves that were feared on land and sea. Seawolves were known to wander away from the pack and stalk farm animals. Even edible sea creatures were not safe. These unique wolves were a constant nuisance to farmers and fishers alike. When the young girls' mothers had learned that a Seawolf was killed, she was greatly relieved because she lived near a river.

*****

As Brehira lay in her bed, the Goddess Dahlia appeared before her dressed in white and upon her head was a crown of gold. Her voice was soft but commanding as she spoke.

"Brehira, I have chosen you to become my first priestess in the new world. You are to select from among your people those with great character to teach and train them in the faith."

"Yes, Goddess," Brehira heard herself say, though her eyes were still closed.

"Open your eyes."

Brehira sat up in bed and there, in mid-air, stood the goddess. At that very moment, a holy book, white with the gold seal of the faith, appeared before her. She hardly had time to gasp at the book when a sword and shield that was so bright appeared.

"Give these to Celio and tell him that Raziel, the god of leadership, law, and order, wishes for him to become his Holy Templar."

Brehira frowned. "Yes, Goddess, but what about my son, Dinary?"

"I have not forgotten Dinary. Another of us has great plans for him," the goddess assured her.

Brehira thanked the goddess for bestowing such honor upon her and her son. The next day, Brehira packed the holy book, sword, and shield and thanked Ndornah, Meletah, and Priestess Diana for their favors and gracious hospitality. Three guards volunteered to escort Brehira back to her ship. But before Brehira left, she gave a gift of a very expensive gem to the high priestess.

Priestess Diana was very pleased. She marveled over the gem and said that the gift would serve as a life-long bond between them.

While Brehira strolled to the ship, the three guards stopped abruptly.

"Is something wrong? Why have we stopped?" Brehira asked.

"You're taking us with you."

"What are you talking about? I thought this was a woman's paradise, why would you want to leave?"

"You need to let us come with you."

"I'm sorry, but I can't. We just can't let people come onto the ship without clearing it with my husband and the captain. I'm afraid it's out of the question."

One of the guards told Brehira that they weren't asking her, they were telling her. She explained that they wanted to leave Domari and explore the realm for themselves. She also explained that it was no animal that had frightened the girls, but men from her ship. And if they had told that to the high Priestess, every man on her ship would be dead right now.

"I don't believe you," Brehira blurted.

"We figured you'd say that," the guard said. She led Brehira to a mass grave and told her to peek in. When Brehira leaned over the freshly dug grave and recognized the men from her ship, she grabbed her chest.

"Dear goddess."

"So, you see why you're taking us with you?"

"Yes."

"And you see, if you tell this to your gesgea and captain, they won't refuse?"

"Yes, again," Brehira sighed and said. "Well, it seems I've made three new friends whose names I don't know."

One of the guards pointed to herself, "I'm Letty; this is Pryah, and that's Alema."

Brehira took the women aboard ship and explained everything to Gangus, Judian, and the Captain. The news spread throughout the ship. No one blamed the women. Many were grateful to the Domarians for their lives and praised the women for keeping the dead sailor's betrayal from their Priestess. And as far as all were concerned, the three men got what they deserved.

Brehira also shared with Dinary and Gangus what the goddess Dahlia had revealed to her. Then she made her way down to Celio's quarters and knocked on his door. "It's Brehira, Celio."

"Lady Abram," he said. "Come in."

She told him her vision and handed him the heavy bundle. Celio placed the bundle on the table and uncovered it. When he saw the gifts, he held his breath. "So, it wasn't a dream after all," and he smiled widely.

Brehira walked out of the room, leaving Celio smoothing his hands over the sword and shield in amazement. The glare of it lit up the entire room.

Chapter Eleven

Land of the Dragon

Weeks passed, and the Cristofur had finally reached the shore line of what would later be known as the City of Jinelle. The Domarians had Brehira to inform captain Dordrecht to stay closer to the shoreline so they could recognize the location where they should disembark.

There, forming in the evening sky, dark smoke hovered and slowly appeared to shape into an eerie being, but it was just a trick of the imagination Dinary thought as he stood gazing up at it. Then he turned his head quickly as ear piercing screams rang out. Up high to the right of him, giant wings, nearly as broad as the Cristofur, flapped like ship sails beating against a strong wind. Between the wings was a long, dark body with a head that appeared to be vomiting fire. The fire-monster was on a rampage, and it was killing and destroying everything in its path. Even from that distance, Dinary could see the outline of its rough, scaly exterior with ridges along its back. Its long tail tipped with arrow shape spikes, and upon its head were two horns. As the terrorized humanoids screamed and trampled one another, the monster continued to shoot forth fire. The blaze burst forth like a stream of burning water as it consumed buildings, farmlands, cattle and frightened souls running for their lives. Wild animals looked like balls of fire with legs as they stampeded towards a nearby lake.

"Great gods of mercy…do you see that?" Celio said joining Dinary on the first upper deck after the sights and screams had alerted him also. The two stood in amazement for a moment, appearing shocked and not quite knowing what to do.

Dinary exhaled hard. "We have to help those poor people."

"What…from that thing?"

"We've got to try," Dinary said, running ahead of him and skipping every other step as he scurried down the stairs.

Celio became annoyed. "Well, wait up, will you! It's not like we're going to a fire! Holy gods…we *are* going to a fire, dragon fire."

As they turned a corner at the bottom of the stairs, they ran into Gangus, almost knocking him to the floor.

"Whoa!" Gangus cautioned.

Dinary and Celio never stopped running as Dinary yelled over his shoulder, "Father call the men to arms, there's a fire-breathing monster attacking some people, and…and we have to help them!"

"Fire-breathing what?"

Not long after Dinary made that statement, the entire ship flew into action. Gangus grabbed his staff, Celio pulled his sword and shield from under his bed, Dinary reached for his sword—his necklace growing warm on his chest, and the Domari warriors, Letty, Pryah, and Alema, also grabbed their swords, spears, and shields.

"Celio," Gangus called, "you stay back and take charge guarding the ship."

"Aye, Aye, Captain," he said mockingly with a disappointing frown.

The Bowman and swordsmen met them on deck, and all climbed into row boats to make their way to shore. By the time they reached land, the fire-monster had gone. All that was left were burning buildings, smoking fields, and suffering animals. The victims of the monster's rage who were alive knelt weeping over their dead as smoke seeped from their charred bodies. The Volarians would soon realize that they were on Timbakni land. Timbaknis were resourceful, honorable, and very religious. They had no use for magic. But they were in for a big surprise. A race of people that the Timbaknis had never met had stepped upon their land with skills and divine powers to face the Timbaknis' deadliest foe.

When Gangus and his warriors came upon the grieving people, they were immediately taken aback by their non-Volarian appearance. They appeared Volarians from the neck down, but from the neck up they resembled a golden-face wolf with a dark wet nose and raised ears on either side of their heads. Gangus looked over at Pryah and gestured for her to come to him. "Do they understand your language?" he whispered.

"Many tribal spokesmen, especially priests, speak several languages."

With that, Gangus turned and said, "We apologize for the intrusion, but we saw from our ship that you were in trouble and came as quickly as we could to help. Sorry, we did not make it in time."

A Timbakni male stepped forward dressed in a long, loose-fitting white robe with green headgear to shield his head from the sun. Most times Timbaknis wore veils to protect their faces from the blowing sand.

"Thank you," the male said. I am Hayman, the high priest of Jinelle. I am glad that you were too late, or I would be burying you and your men as well." Embarrassed after seeing Letty, Pryah, and Alema, he faked clearing his throat, "and women," he said, politely nodding.

Relieved that they understood each other, Gangus introduced himself and all who were with him. Hayman was naturally curious about the staff, and he asked about it. Gangus wisely didn't reveal its power but said that it was only good for keeping an old man steady on his feet. Then after seeing the extent of the injuries, Gangus sent Lygone back to the ship to bring Celio, Brehira and some of the women to help ease the suffering. Then he and his men assisted with disposing of the bodies.

Brehira was a remarkable woman who had often thought of herself as an ordinary, flesh and blood Volarian female whose only obligation was to marry, love her husband, bear children and to serve her people as best she could. She had always been quite satisfied with that existence, but now these unexpected spiritual gifts frightened her. Gangus spent that night giving her wise counseling and comforting her. Little did she know how soon her gifts would be greatly needed.

As they waited for Lygone to return, Hayman took them underground to where the Timbaknis lived. They only came up to attend to their cattle and farmlands, Hayman told them, and to fetch water. Every month for years, many of them died fighting to protect their water and food supply from the evil menacing beast Hayman called a Drake. He said Drakes had existed in the land for centuries, but that his ancestors had rid the land of them, they thought; but, twenty years ago, they emerged again. Some said that the adult Drakes knew they were dying out and had hidden their eggs and that the hatchlings had eaten one another until one was strong enough to survive on its own. "No one knows fully," Hayman said, "just speculations." They entered a long hallway that was dim and cold.

"So, you think there's just one Drake left?" Gangus asked.

"Yes, and it's the biggest and toughest anyone of us has ever seen. We've done everything, including poisoning our cattle, hoping to kill it. But not even the deadliest poison can phase it."

"But, this is a realm full of powers. We've seen it with our own eyes in the land of Gorr."

"Oh, no. We are servants of our god. We don't engage in sorcery," Hay-

85

man said shaking his head.

"But not all power is sorcery."

"No good thing can come of magic," Hayman said, gazing at the staff.

Gangus thought quickly as not to lose the Timbaknis' hospitality. "Oh, you need not worry about this staff. It's quite harmless; I can assure you," Gangus said trying to laugh it off. Gangus thought of Brehira and her gifts and wasn't sure if it were wise for the Timbakni to observe her using it for fear they would mistake it for magic. If I could only get them to see that it's a gift from the goddess, he thought.

When they entered the main chambers, Dinary marveled at the beauty of the underground. Colorful rugs covered the floors. Furniture was made of dark painted wood. Rooms were loaded with fine art of sculptures: short ones on tables—tall ones in every corner of the rooms, and lovely portraits of their ancestors lined the stone walls. The children were orderly and obedient. The females were stylishly dressed in colorful tunics over long, white robes and wonderfully carved wooden jewelry around their necks and wrists.

Seeing that Hayman was a priest of peace, Gangus signaled to his soldiers that it was all right to leave their weapons outside the main chamber. Gangus, of course, was allowed to keep his staff since, as Hayman believed, it was only a walking stick. If Hayman only knew that the staff was far more powerful and dangerous than all their weapons put together. Gangus decided he would tell this lie to every strange creature of every strange land they came into, so they wouldn't feel so vulnerable and naked if forced to give up their weapons. But, we must not give them up to easily and without a fuss, he thought, for fear they might figure out the real use of the staff.

The Timbaknis treated Volarian guests well; there were tables spread with sweet fruits and vegetables from their trees and gardens—even the water that was so clear tasted sweet. They ate roasted meats and thick yellowish milk that came from a strange animal they'd never seen before. Gangus didn't offer the priest wine. He didn't think it appropriate—knowing the effects of it was unknown to creatures of their realm. And who'd be wicked enough to allow a priest to be seen falling drunk in the midst of his followers? Gangus instructed those who accompanied him not to drink also because they needed to be ready if the Drake should return.

After stuffing themselves, at the insistence of the priest, Gangus and the others settled back and listened to the priest give them the history of the

Timbaknis. He said they had first arrived in Bethica several centuries ago, the first of three great exoduses fleeing a terrible disaster in the west known as The Gloaming. They fought, fled, and traveled across the whole of the southern realms before finally settling in the Amersis Desert, a region where no others had claimed. From there, they built up their strength and tamed the wild jungles along the coast, eventually forging a healthy and stable region of small villages. Recently, there have only been a few border disputes with the Nekanians and the Sucari. "We Timbaknis love to travel. We are very adventurous creatures, but dangers abroad and near, keep us planted in our land, I'm afraid," Hayman concluded.

"Near, you mean the Drake," Gangus inquired.

"Yes. That blasted Evil."

"Why don't you just leave?" Dinary asked.

Hayman frowned. "Leave our land? Never. No bloody beast is going to force us from our homes. Why, our ancestor's bones would cry out from the dirt. Our generation would be a disgrace to them."

Just then, a Timbakni boy came running into the room and whispered to Hayman. Hayman nodded and told him to bring them in. He turned to Gangus. "It seems more of your people are here."

"Ah—it is the Healers that have arrived to help your injured," Gangus responded.

"But our gardens flourish with the best medicinal herbs in the land. Many travel from far regions for our healing herbs. Timbaknis receive much for our trade. What could you possibly add but magic," Hayman said like it was a bad taste in his mouth.

Gangus became uncomfortable and twisted in his chair. He struggled to speak the right words. But before the words spilled from his lips, the Timbakni boy entered and behind him was Celio carrying his shield with a lightning bolt in the middle of a sky-blue disc which is the symbol of Raziel, the god of honor. First, Hayman frowned at the boy for not insisting Celio put aside his weapons, but when Hayman saw the symbol of the god of his ancestors, he better understood the boy's misgivings. Hayman nearly bowed to the shield but managed to stand straight. The corners of his mouth curled up, and his eyes appeared to gleam with gladness. Behind Celio, came Brehira and her ladies. Then, Hayman spoke to Celio.

"Your shield carries the symbol of Raziel, the god I serve."

"I am his Holy Templar."

Hayman's eyes widened, and he turned to Gangus. "Why didn't you tell me?" Before Gangus could answer him, Hayman turned to Celio, Brehira and the women, "Please, you are all welcome to stay as long as you'd like. What is ours is now yours."

Delighted with the turn of events, Gangus stood. "Priest Hayman, this is my wife, Brehira. She is Priestess of Goddess Dahlia."

"Ah—priestess, you are indeed welcome to our abode."

"Thank you so much, Priest Hayman. But if you don't mind, I'd like to get right to helping the injured."

"Oh, yes. Of course. Popi," he said to the Timbakni boy, "take the Priestess to the Sickhall."

Before Brehira attended the sick, she, Gangus and Celio felt it necessary to give a demonstration of her powers and to reveal the conversations she had with Goddess Dahlia. Hayman reluctantly agreed to allow Brehira and her assistants to help and may not have been aware that there had never been any historical evidence of magic healing in any form. Furthermore, great scholars had always agreed that healing was far beyond the deeds of magic.

Brehira and the women followed the young boy out of the chamber and down a short hall—down the stairs to a long hallway that smelled of cooked flesh. Moaning and groaning bodies lay in a row upon high, thick bundles of bulky, bloody bedding. Some were still and had dirty cloth covering their faces like death masks.

*****

While everyone slept, Brehira, her ladies, and the Timbakni healers worked feverishly through the night, cleaning wounds, applying medicinal herbs and bandaging arms, legs, feet, faces and sometimes whole bodies, until they were exhausted. The others took turns napping, but Brehira wouldn't sleep. She now knew her new reason for living; and as much as she loved being a wife and a mother, nothing had ever given her more pleasure in life than bringing comfort and healing to the sick. She could feel the power oozing out of her hands, under the bandages and into the skin and bodies of her patients. She had felt the pulse of the pain that thumped throughout their bodies. And after locating it, she felt when it suddenly stopped at her touch. But her healing powers only lasted a few hours a day. Because of that, she helped a few of her patients with traditional medicines. Therefore, the overall healing of the skin, bones, and tissues would take a day longer.

Meanwhile, the Timbaknis marveled at the clothes the Volarian women wore. When Gangus saw how much they delighted in them, he sent Lygone back for silk cloth and cashmere goats—pearls for the females and gold for the males. The Timbaknis, though their garments were simple, were very style conscious. They had longed to be noted for their way of dressing. And these new Volarian clothes and jewelry would quickly bring their wishes to reality.

Days turned into weeks and knowledge of Brehira's healing powers spread throughout the Timbakni land. The injured that were blind due to scorched eyes could now see. Brehira and team mended broken leg and ankle bones. The cooked flesh showed total healing, and bandages removed from legs, hands, and arms—even necks and faces showed no scarring. The injured looked as if no Drake attacked took place.

While Brehira had led the healers in treating the wounded souls, a small group of Volarians, led by Gangus, worked from dawn to dust helping to re-store buildings; searching and rounding up scared off cattle, and salvaging fruit and vegetables from badly scorched trees and fields. As Priest Hayman nailed a plank of wood into the barn roof, Gangus questioned him about the Drake and where he could find it. Hayman's hammer stopped midway a bang.

"You're not thinking about going after the Drake?" Hayman muttered.

"We're not doing all of this repairing and healing just to leave and have that blasted beast come back and attack you again."

"But it's usually months before it comes back. I hate to tell you this, but the Drake doesn't just kill, but consider us its preferred food. It only eats the animals when we manage to escape it."

"And you're fine with that?"

"Of course we're not fine with it. As you can see, our mates and children are safe. We try to fight it off the best we can, hoping it will take one or two animals from the herd and then leave."

"And Timbaknis have lived like this for how long?"

"Over twenty years," Hayman said, lowering his head as if he finally felt ashamed. Then he lifted the hammer and drove a nail in the plank so hard the wood cracked.

When darkness came, the men stopped working and settled in for the night. Gangus continued to badger Hayman about the Drake—its habits, its escape routes if it attacked at night, noon, morning, how early—how late? And where he thought it resided when it wasn't attacking. But Hayman continued to resist giving Gangus the information he wanted. He liked his new friends and didn't want them killed and eaten. The Drake had already taken enough from him—his brother and sister, his boyhood friends, even some of his fellow priests. No. No more, he thought. But Gangus was determined not to leave that bloody beast alive. He felt that the Timbaknis were an exceptional people and that they deserved to live Drake free.

Much later on, around day break, Gangus woke to shouts outside his chamber. He covered himself and hurried out to see about the commotion. He rushed in and saw Hayman, Dinary and a few others half-circling Nazi, one of the soldiers that were left guarding the ship. The soldier sat sweating and panting, his clothes discolored with dark smudges. Brehira handed the guard a cup of water. Gangus stepped quickly up to him. "Nazi, what is it? What's wrong? Is everyone all right back at the ship?"

Brehira looked over at her husband, and he read her face. Gangus' shoulders slumped at the dull in her usually bright eyes.

Nazi took a final gulp of his water. "Lord Abram…there was nothing… we could do. We shot arrows and everything at that beast." He took in a deep breath, "… and it attacked the ship. The fire roared above our heads. There was nothing we could do, sir." Nazi dropped his head, and Brehira padded him on the shoulder.

"Merciful gods," Hayman said looking at Gangus.

"But was anyone hurt?" Gangus asked.

"That's just it, sir. It only attacked the sails. Like it wanted us to stay until it returned or something, and…and it knew we couldn't go anywhere. We finally got the fire out. But this thing acted like it could think. We shot arrows at it, but it wouldn't attack us, just the sails."

"Drakes are brilliant…even humorous at times," Hayman said. "They like toying with their food."

"Well, at least no one got hurt. But we have extra sails," Gangus assured everyone, looking around. He didn't want them to worry or think things were hopeless.

"It destroyed everything that held the sails, sir."

Gangus shut his eyes tight and ran his fingers through his dark hair. "Of course, everything is made of wood...how stupid of me."

"I'm sorry, sir. We never fought anything like this before. I'm afraid we're stuck here." He lowered his head.

Gangus stepped closer to him and placed a hand on his shoulder. "You're an excellent soldier, Nazi. I'm very proud of you. I doubt if we could have done anything more if we'd been there."

Nazi's face brightened. "Oh, thank you, sir."

Brehira grabbed Nazi gently under his arm. "I'll take him back and give him something so he can sleep." She and the guard disappeared into the darkness outside the chamber.

"I'm so sorry, Lord Abram," Hayman expressed.

Gangus rubbed his tired eyes. "It couldn't be helped I suppose. There's nothing more we can do tonight anyway. If you'll excuse me, I'll return to bed."

"But, what are we going to do?" Dinary asked.

As Gangus exited the chamber, his answer got caught up in his yawn. "We'll talk about it another time."

Dinary seemed surprised at his father's calm behavior after hearing about the attack. He, Celio and the others soon returned to their beds, but no one slept soundly—no one except Nazi who Brehira had heavily sedated.

A few days passed. Gangus never talked about the ship attack as he'd promised Dinary he would. However, he did continue to pester the priest about the Drake. One fine day, after a full morning of Gangus' relentless questioning, Hayman felt like a beaten rag and finally revealed to him everything he knew or had heard about the Drake. If Gangus had been a dog, his ears would have perked straight up on his head; that's just how thrilled he was. Thank the gods, Gangus said under his breath, because his plan 'B' was to get Hayman drunk with wine, then question him. But he wasn't sure how to keep Brehira from finding out. Priest and priestess could not act unseemly, because of the sacredness of the priesthood.

*****

It had been several weeks since the Timbaknis welcomed the Volarians. Many injured made a full recovery while some that were near death needed a few more rest days. Volarians and Timbakni worked side-by-side repairing many buildings, and though fruit trees and farmlands had been severely torched, loads of fruit and vegetables were gathered in deep push-barrels and stored in underground chamber bends. Volarian swordsmen mercifully killed the suffering animals. Still, a day had arrived that Priest Hayman dreaded; Gangus had drilled Hayman over and over about the Drake and had planned to seek and kill the beast that had caused the Timbaknis so much heartache.

It had been a long work day for all. The Timbakni females and their children had turned in for the night, while some of their mates sat with the Volarians to plan a strategy to destroy the Drake. Priest Hayman sat across from Gangus while the others listened. "I hope you know what you're doing, Gangus," Hayman said, scratching several places on his body. This scratching appeared an ongoing grooming ritual that the Timbaknis had to perform periodically to keep the insects from nesting in their fur. It annoyed Gangus to no end, though he tried not to show it. "I'm not underestimating your ability, but many have tried to kill the thing and have died or lived to regret it." He bent and scratched his ankle, then sat up. "Let's suppose you and your warriors get lucky and kill the Drake, which I doubt, where are you going to go from here?"

Now that the scratching was over, Gangus made eye contact. "The Domarians," he said nodding to them, "are taking my people to some unoccupied land just north of you, near a great lake. There are hundreds of us, and we tend to settle there. Of course, now we'll have to travel by foot. Can you tell me more about the land?"

"Yes, I believe I can. The area is beautiful, full of rolling hills, grass fields, thick forest with small edible game, and a lake for fishing. It has two seasons like we have. Wet, which is very hot and Dry, which is very cool."

"Then why isn't it occupied?" Gangus inquired.

"Sounds like something's wrong," Dinary weighed in.

"You're right, young Dinary. The Drake destroyed it over a hundred years ago. It took the land just that long to restore itself. Nobody will live there. Some say the gods caused the Drake to destroy the land because the people were wicked and served fallen Angels instead of the gods. But that's probably just a folk tale."

"Well, fine," Dinary said. "Then all we have to do is kill the blasted beast and the land is ours."

Hayman's dark eyes dotted back and forth as if he pondered what to say next. "Have any of you ever fought a Drake before?" There was complete silence. "That's what I thought," Hayman said leaning forward in his chair. "Even if you kill it, there's still the Badlands. It is called Badlands for a reason. Living underground protects us, but your people will be out in the open, where everything and anything can get at them. And there are many unknown things in the Badlands."

"What sort of things?" Gangus asked with raised eyebrows.

Hayman pulled on his chin. "Let me give you an option first before telling you about the Badlands." He blew out a small gust of breath and placed both hands on his knees. "There are three ways to get to the land you want to settle. The safest," he said, "is to start from Vaslof, southwest of here. It's safe because it's an open trail with no forest, therefore nothing to hide behind or jump out from to harm you, just a straight shot."

"All right, it sounds good so far," Gangus said. "But you're not finished, are you?"

Hayman dropped his head and looked at Gangus from under his lashes. "It's the longest. While there's nothing or anyone to harm you, there's also no water for hundreds of miles and your people and animals will die of thirst."

"Well, that's out!" Dinary said. "Now number two."

"That would be Lothian. It is shorter, but you'd have to cut through the thick forest. The trail won't be easy on foot. And it is a little more dangerous. The forest is dark even in the day time. You won't see them, but the Seawolves will see you, and they'll kill you and eat your animals."

Everyone looked at each other and braced themselves for number three. "So, now I'll tell you about the Badlands. The Badlands is the quickest way, but it's the most dangerous. Right now, you're in Jinell. It is only a few hundred miles from where you wish to settle. It should take you just a month of travel."

"BUT?" Gangus blurted.

"BUT… it is where the menacing Goblins live, underground, like us. They are not killers, but they're notorious thieves. They can steal the gold right out of your mouth while you're sleeping and wouldn't break a snore. Not only that, the land itself is a bit of a booby trap, quick sand, deep, irregular slopes, steep hills, and full of the deadliest serpents in the whole region." Hayman paused.

"AND," Gangus asked wisely.

93

"AND…" he appeared to deflate. "It's where you'll find the Drake deep within its cave. And I do mean deep. Lord Abram, I've never heard of anyone coming out of that cave alive. So, now make your choice."

There was a short silence—as if everyone present was still trying to digest all that Priest Hayman had fed them. They buzzed among themselves for minutes at a time. Then Celio spoke up with, "I say, we kill this bloody thing and take our chances in the Badlands." The room began to buzz again, and some nodded in agreement with Celio. Then Pryah spoke up. "Lord Abram, I'm so sorry we brought you and your people here. We didn't know about the Drake, honestly. I'm sure we can find other lands. Perhaps…"

"No," Gangus interrupted her. "This is the land the gods spoke of. I'm sure of it. We will kill the Drake. No matter how long it takes."

"Yeah, that's right, absolutely, you darn right," were just some of the words Gangus heard coming from his warriors. Others grinned and nodded to Gangus with approval.

Hayman sat back and shook his head. "As I said, I sure hope you know what you're doing."

Gangus reached over and touched Hayman on the knee. "I know you're worried about us. And no, we've never fought a Drake before. But you're good people. You shouldn't have to live in fear of this thing. I believe the gods will be with us."

Priest Hayman smiled and placed his hand upon Gangus' hand. "I think I'm starting to believe you, Lord Abram. Something tells me you're just the man to do it. May the gods bless all of you. I wish I could go with you. But, I'm afraid I wouldn't be much good." He chuckled softly.

"Your prayers are what we need from you."

He grabbed Gangus' shoulder and shook it slightly. "And you shall have them, Lord Abram. My priests and I will fast until you and your soldiers leave for the Badlands."

"It's most appreciative."

Late in the night, as all slept, Gangus, Dinary, Celio and the Domarians stayed up putting together a battle strategy. It lasted until almost dawn.

Chapter Twelve

The Mouth of the Dragon

Gangus and his men, along with Dinary and his top four field command-ers: Celio, Lygone, Olutunji, and Ricus were in a good mood before the battle and had no doubts about victory. But planning to leave their armor behind had nothing to do with their confidence. Nor were they stupid. Their armor contained metal, and one blast of fire from the Drake could fuse the metal with their flesh. Nazi, still furious over the loss of the ship, was promoted to Commander of the fifth regiment. He was a skilled fighter and had fought fearlessly against the demons of the ghost ship.

It took only a few days to plan the battle. Gangus' men were well trained in archery, spear-throwing, hand-to-hand combat and small one-on-one skir-mishes. They had fought the undead, and a demon possessed fifty-foot wood carving of a pagan god. Nothing Gangus said could prepare them for the bat-tle against the near invincible fire-breathing Drake. Nevertheless, his strategy was simple: Weapons aimed at the softest spots, the eyes, nose, opened mouth, and belly, proved more effective. The archers and spear throwers would stand high on a cave ledge or outside hill and shoot low; Gangus would be out front with his staff, which each spell only functioned ten times daily, so he'd have to make every blow count. Celio would stand behind Gangus. And Dinary and swordsmen would position themselves behind Celio. Swords are help-less against fire, but Drakes need a few minutes for their bodies to refuel; so, swordsmen would have to move in quickly—do as much damage as possible and move back. Also, moving in meant they'd be in danger of its claws and tail. Steel cannot pierce the scales, but there is just enough opening between scales for the steel to slip in, hit a vital organ, or draw blood. Celio will use his shield which is the only shield that dragon fire can't melt. His shield will protect swordsman every time they move back after attacking. Letty, Pryah, and Alema would be sent back to help guard the ship in case the Drake escaped. The rest would be in the hands of the gods.

Gangus was proud of his men. They were loyal, mentally tough and strong. Every part of their body was lean and muscular. When they weren't fighting, Gangus gave them heavy physical labor to keep them in shape. Today, he told them to double their mental capacity and trust in Gailzur, the fierce god of war.

Before the dawn broke, the men marched off under a blanket of darkness. Across the desert, they could hear the sand creatures, each singing their familiar song. Or were they betraying the men with rhythmic warnings –watching as they marched into an ambush? These are crazy notions soldiers get just before a battle. Gangus and his men were no different. Quietly, they inched slowly across the beige sand, some in the region called, the god's dust. Nothing stirred but the wind. There were no tracks to follow; the wind made sure of that. On the way back their footsteps will have vanished—brushed away by the internal broom of the gods. Up ahead, the men saw prints, not foot prints, but body prints of serpents. Celio shuttered at the thought of being bitten. He wasn't afraid, but that he was a soldier and soldiers died in battle—not doubled up in a fetal position on the sand floor from a serpent bite.

They had walked for hours, stepping over animals and other creature caucuses. They saw fragments of long abandon caravans. As they marched deeper inside the Badlands, the stench of death and strange, eerie sounds surrounded them. Stranger yet, small creatures they'd never seen before scurried by them. Others hid behind thick bushes and stared out at them.

Gangus gave Dinary a command. "Halt!" Dinary shouted. "We'll camp here!" Every right foot hit the ground hard on cue. The men were instructed to set up camp.

"Can you believe we're camping here?" Lygone asked Ricus.

Ricus chuckled. "What's the matter, scared you, baby?"

Lygone waved him away and continued setting up and putting things in place for food, and rest. It was still daylight, and some were encouraged to take naps so they could stay awake and guard the others against the thieving Goblins as they slept through the night. Then hours before daybreak, they would be relieved so they could be well rested at dawn when the traveling would continue all the way to the cave.

*****

The entrance to the cave engulfed them with impenetrable darkness. Gangus watched their shadows dissolve into the blackness as they slowly moved inside. Torches were lit and mounted along the trail. The men readied their

96

weapons. The brown rock path led them deeper into the throat of the cavern. The rock walls were jagged with sharp edges like blades. From the ceiling, there hung stalactites and blood sucking bird roosts. As they entered the long oval tunnel, thick musky air filled their lungs and clogged their throats—but not one stopped moving. "Halt!" The men stopped and braced themselves. In the thick darkness up ahead, were ruby, red rocks set far apart from each other. Gangus held up his hand to the men to stay as he stepped forward to get a better look at the rocks.

"I've been waiting for you!" said a growling voice from behind the red eyes glaring at him. The Drake reared its mighty head and vomited out a blazing sea that heated the cave instantly like a scorching desert. Gangus thrust the staff forward with both hands. "Drabeck!" The staff globe glowed and shot out a wind block that held the fiery sea so strongly that the blaze curled and flooded backward over the Drake's head. As Gangus held the blaze, the men got into position. Bowmen and lance throwers climbed and stood high on a ledge, arrows and lance pointing. Celio stood behind him and Dinary and swordsmen behind Celio. Gangus could feel the wind dying down and began backing up. While the Drake paused to refuel, twenty steel-tipped arrows cut loose striking the Drake in the tongue and gums and knocking out several teeth. The lance flew down but just missed its eye by a few inches as the Drake moved its head. Pain from steel was something the Drake had never felt before. And the wind from the staff was something it had never encountered as well. That made the beast to rethink its battle strategy. Perhaps, take the battle outside. Strike from so far up in the air rendering their puny weapons useless. Then through a hail of arrows, the Drake spit forth again, consuming the arrows in mid-air. The Drake tried to back them out of the cave with its fire, but Gangus thrust the staff forward again, and the winds blew back the flames. Immediately Dinary, with his necklace glowing, ran forward and rammed his blade between the scales, hitting a vital organ. His men followed with blades slashing, slicing part of its clawed toes, and cutting into its belly. The Drake cursed at them as the blood flowed from its belly, foot, and mouth. The wind ceased. The Drake had figured out the staff's timing and had held back some of its fuel. It cut loose a lesser, yet, still deadly blaze, but Celio jumped up front and held the blaze with his shield. For several minutes the Drake fought helplessly against the staff, the shield, and the arrows until finally, an accurately thrown lance took out an eye. The Drake was enraged, and its roar shook the cave so that the walls and ceiling cracked causing huge rocks to fall upon three of the soldiers, killing them instantly. The rumble of the cave also jarred the staff from Gangus' hand that landed several feet from him. Then the Drake bolted, mowing over the men and leaving several dead in its path. Gangus yelled, "Beckon," extending his hands forward towards the staff and it flew into his hands, but it was too late, the Drake had exited the cave.

Gangus ordered the injured to stay back while he and the rest followed the Drake to the outside. As soon as they stepped outside the cave, they saw the Drake when it scooped up Celio with its mouth and flew high into the sky. Celio forced his shield between its upper and lower teeth to keep the Drake from biting down and kept slashing away at its tongue that tried to push the shield away. Finally, the Drake's saliva was making its teeth slip further down the shield, and the tip of a tooth was cutting his head and shoulder. Then a rumbling sound from the Drake's throat signaled it was going to blow fire. Celio knew he had to jump, though he wouldn't survive the drop. But he was determined not to be eaten or burned to death, so he dived out falling to the ground at tremendous speed, leaving his sword and shield. With only a few feet until he smashed into the ground below, Celio made his peace with his god and closed his eyes. He thought about his beautiful wife and all the children they would not have. As his body soared downward, a stream of blue reached out and caught him, slowing his descent to that of a floating feather. Celio opened his eyes and followed the blue stream to Gangus' staff that was pointing right at him. The blue placed him on the ground like a mother would place a child in its crib. Celio sat panting and half-smiling when a bright light glared from the ground, and his sword and shield appeared.

The men pointed to the sky and cheered as the Drake, half-clawed—wings heavy with arrows, a sea of blood dripping from it, and a lance protruding from its eye, fluttered away into the distance like a drunken bird.

*****

Back at Jinelle, Brehira was busy healing the sick, when Popi came running into her, hopping up and down and blurting something, but because of his excitement, she couldn't make out what he was saying. So, she followed him, but stop mid-way when something caught her ear. It was singing. She yelled, "They did it…thank the gods!"

The Chronicles of Bethica

Her shouting brought everyone to her. "They did it…it's done."

Hayman entered the chamber. "Priestess, is something wrong?"

"No. Priest Hayman, everything is right. The Drake is no more."

"Are you sure…how do you know?" He paused as she and her women stood grinning from ear to ear.

Hayman strained his ear. "What's all that singing?"

"That's what I'm trying to tell you. That's the Volarian victory song. They only sing it when they've won."

The singing got closer, and Brehira ran out with others on her heels. They stood waving at the men who were covered with blood, holding up the injured that could walk and carrying those who couldn't. The song rang out of every mouth—no matter how injured.

Volarian men
will go through thick and thin
to carry out the will
of our god.

Protect friend and kin
and will fight to the end
casting out all evil
where it trod.

No better men than we
as we travel sea to sea
beating every shadow
into dust.

We shall shun iniquity
while claiming victory
in the god
that we all trust

Oh…We'll keep fighting dawn to dust
for the god that we all trust
The god of gods
Mighty Lord Raziel.

The god of gods
Mighty Lord Raziel.

The crowd ran out to greet them with kisses and hugs. Brehira hugged Gangus and Dinary. Then kissed Celio and as many men as she could. Priest Hayman had tears in his eyes. He grabbed Gangus and bear-hugged him. The soldiers followed the crowd down into the underground. More songs and cheers rang up to the sky.

Miles away, deep in the bowels of Bethica, resided an unknown cave. Inside, giant skeletal frames spread as far as several miles long. The Drake, barely crawling, managed to drag itself to one particular skeletal head, perhaps its mother, perhaps not. It laid its battered face upon the skull and took its last breath. Its black soul soared into the abyss.

Chapter Thirteen

The Divine and the Evil

As soon as the other nearby villages heard the news that the Volarians soldiers had defeated the Drake, for days on end, a great celebration broke out all over Jinelle. Right away, the real story was shunned for a more thrilling one that would delight the children at bedtime. As it was told—Gangus was said to have jumped on the Drake's back while it flew hundreds of feet into the air and gouged out its eye while hanging from its horns. And brave soldiers, while on fire, were said to have fought the Drake for several minutes before they died. People also said that the Drake pleaded on its knees for its life, as Gangus yelled, "Did you show Timbakni mercy you dreaded beast?" and drove a spear straight through its heart. Gangus thought the songs were ridiculous, and he tried many times to tell the real story, but the fake one took on a life of its own and spread throughout the land.

Soon a day Priest Hayman had dreaded was upon him. He had to say goodbye to Gangus. "You have done a great service for my people, my dear friend." He held Gangus by both shoulders. "We will never forget this. If there is ever anything me or my people can do for you, it will not go undone, as the gods are my witnesses." He kissed Gangus on both cheeks and tapped him lightly on the shoulder. Gangus smiled and humbly nodded.

After all, they had encountered since boarding the Cristofur from the little village at Skatts Island, Five hundred and nineteen settlers, three hundred and thirty soldiers, one captain and a one hundred and sixty man crew stood to begin the journey to the Promised Land. As the people held on to their belongings, they watched Gangus and Brehira say their goodbyes. There were tears and hugs, and gifts exchanged and promises to meet up again in the future. With last-minute waves, the caravan set out for the promised paradise.

As his dear friend, Priest Hayman had warned, the Badlands was still a great deal dangerous even without the Drakes' presence, and the wiser choice was to avoid the Badlands and travel on the outskirts near the ocean. But though that would bring them to the land safer, it would not be the quickest route. It would take three and a half weeks to reach the land, and there was only enough food and water for fourteen days. They would have to cut through the Badlands to reach the west side of the land where they could quickly replenish themselves with fish from the lake and small game from the nearby forest.

As they entered the Badlands, Gangus took the lead with Celio behind and Dinary leading his men with Lygone, captain of the swordsmen, by his side. Olutunji marched ahead of his lancers, Kofius—in front of his archers, Nazi was Rear Captain, and the Domarian warriors took charge of the detail to guard the single women and took personal charge of guarding their tents at night. Well into the Badlands, the trouble began. They had to stop several times so Brehira and her women could heal poisoned bites from two-headed serpents, flying lizards, and hairy insects that made high-pitched noises. After the last stop, Gangus ordered that they camp.

A few hours later, Gangus entered Captain Dordrecht's tent. "Well, is everything all right?"

Dordrecht turned from his mirror—his lips and face surrounded by a white cloud. He held the razor just an inch from his face. "Couldn't be better," he said, lifting his chin and pulling the razor upward his throat.

Gangus stood watching him balloon his cheek to get a cleaner and smoother slide. "Ah, do you mind?" Dordrecht asked, looking at Gangus in the mirror.

Gangus frowned.

"I need the light," Dordrecht said.

"Oh, sorry," Gangus said, moving away from the opening of the tent.

Dordrecht finished shaving, splashed water on his face then grabbed a towel. He walked towards Gangus—wiping his face then tossed the towel on a bench. "You always carry that thing?" he asked, nodding towards the staff.

"Remember what happened the last time I left it about?"

"Oh, yes," Dordrecht said chuckling. "Have a seat."

"Actually, I only stopped by for a minute. Just wanted to see if you had any regrets."

"About coming, you mean? None whatsoever. Is that the real reason you stopped by? I can assure you; I'm not about to turn back."

"Well…that and the fact that if you do decide to stick around and be a part of us. I'd like for you to take charge as merchant and trader of our goods. We're bringing a lot of goods to this land that can be used for the betterment of Bethica. We'll need right away to set up trading and to find out what's out there for us. We're not giving our goods, especially our knowledge of steel making, for trinkets. We need to know what is out there in Bethica that can benefit our race."

"I see. Well, I'm flattered. And I accept." He grabbed Gangus' hand and shook it. "I'll do my best."

"Good. I'm glad you're remaining with us. So, I'll talk with you soon." Gangus left the tent.

They had spent four days in camp and Olutunji had come back with more bad news that the small game and plants were not safe for consumption, at least not good for Volarian consumption. And the water was stagnant and full of yellowish slime. They would have to keep moving and eat smaller rations.

One day after the morning meal, there came shouts from the men, "Halt where you are!" Gangus bolted out of his tent in the directions of the commotion; all of his men stood with weapons aimed at the intruders. Gangus with staff in hand walked forward. "What do you want?"

"Nothing of yours, Lord Abram." The little creature said in broken acacia.

"You know my name?" Gangus said in Gurkin, the language of Goblins, Orcs, and HobGoblins.

Aye, you speak our tongue. Good, said the Goblin. "And it is hard not to know your name. Aren't you the one who destroyed the fire-breathing, monster, Lord Abram?"

Dinary who was standing back walked into view of the intruders, the sun at his back. "You Goblins are a long way from your territory," he said in Gurkin. "You must want something!"

Celio eased out from another shadow. "Say what it is and be gone with you," he commanded.

Gangus held up his hand, for the men to hold their peace. "If you want nothing, then why are you here?"

"We desire no trouble. We just wanted to make sure you and your soldiers were not going to present more problems for our people."

"What problems?"

"You destroyed our Drake. That's a problem for us now."

"Why is that a problem? We did you and this whole region a favor."

"Lord Abram, I'm sorry to have to rain on your heroic reputation. But not everyone is better off without the Drake. You see, the Drake was no danger to us because we live underground and our food source and water supply are underground. The Drake was our protection. Now that it's gone, all of our enemies who once stayed away because of the Drake, are back and now entering our region, attacking us and stealing our supplies. Our survival is no longer certain. So, we are here to command a favor. We believe you owe us."

Gangus relaxed and looked more sympathetically at the head Goblin. "You want me and my men to rid you of your enemies?"

"As I said, Lord Abram. I believe you owe us."

"Let me discuss this with my commanders. In three days, return to us, and I'll have your answer."

"Thank you, Lord Abram. In three days, then." Every soldier's eye held tight to the Goblins until they were well out of camp and out of sight.

Celio couldn't believe the nerve of them. Putting both hands on his hips, he nodded to Gangus. "Yeah, and while we're all here talking it over, they'll be somewhere planning to rob and kill us."

"So true, if these creatures 'are' the same as the ones from our home land, they definitely can't be trusted, but I think they're sincere in this," Gangus reasoned.

"Father is right. Although these creatures appear inferior to the ones we fought back home. They're not trustworthy, but they're not stupid either. They'd never take us on."

Brehira weighed in smiling. "No, they wouldn't dare attack the great Lord Abram who jumped on the back of the mighty Drake as it flew a thousand miles into the air and gouged out its eye with his finger while holding on to its nose." The men howled with laughter at Brehira's teasing. They knew Gangus hated that tale and was annoyed that children delighted in the song. But Gangus had to admit to himself that the song was funny, and so he laughed too.

*****

Two and a half days had passed, and the men still had not agreed on the Goblins. Gangus thought it wise to help them. He wanted to forge friendships with as many beings in this new land as were possible. But Celio felt it was a trick to get all of the men bogged down fighting their enemies and leave the camp with women and children only half protected. Dinary, arguing hard against his father, sided with Celio.

"Father, how do we know that these so-called enemy creatures haven't always been here? The Goblins are liars."

Celio could be hotheaded, but he adored Gangus like a father, though Gangus was only twelve years older. His disagreements with Gangus were always very subtle. "Lord Abram," he said in a soft voice, "with all due respect, sir, I've never questioned your judgment. But I think it would be a mistake to leave our people partially protected and go tramping around out there on some wild goose chase."

"We owe the Goblins nothing. Let them fight their own battles," Nazi scoffed. Nazi wasn't a hothead, but could always be counted on to say what he thought, often with pun intended.

"All right, all right," Gangus said, wiping his brow. "I'll take all of what you say into consideration. I'll be in my tent." He slowly made it into his tent where Brehira sat brushing her long dark mix-grey hair. He loved watching her primp herself. She was still beautiful after all these years. She lay the brush aside and turned to him. "You all right, Love?"

"You think I'm getting old?"

She got up and walked over to him, slid down beside him on their cot and touched his cheek. "I think you're getting better, like a fine wine."

"No. I mean it."

"Honey, why, because Dinary and the men disagreed with you? Even kings have subjects around them to give advice. No king can rule otherwise. But that doesn't mean he's not still king and worthy of rule."

He looked over at her and smiled, taking her hand from his face and holding it. "And let me add that no king can rule effectively without a wise queen by his side." He kissed her hand.

"What they say makes sense, my love, but I trust your reason to resist. What can you tell me that you're not telling them?"

"That we don't know these creatures we're meeting in this new land. No matter how bad they are, if we make friends and not enemies of them, perhaps somewhere down the road we might be able to use them in some capacity."

"In what capacity could we possibly use the Goblins?"

"I don't know. All I know is the gods are not clear on why we're here. And I don't want to make enemies of anyone if I can help it until I find out more from the god's."

"Then why didn't you explain that?"

"Because right now all they know is what I know, that we're here to build a nation that will serve the gods. But I have a feeling the gods want more than for us to serve. And I don't want the people to think that I brought them all out here just to fight and die for some meaningless cause for the gods."

"So you want to help the Goblins just in case we need them later?" Gangus nodded to her.

"Perhaps I can help. Tell the Goblins you'll do it. But unknown to the Goblins, don't take the soldiers…"

"Don't take the soldiers but—"

"Listen, love. Take Dinary and Celio with you. Whatever is out there won't be able to stand against them and your staff. Also, you're taking me."

"What?"

"Let me finish. You know the goddess has gifted me with divine abilities to fight against the powers of darkness, all evil and immorality."

"The goddess is turning my sweet into a one woman army," he said then kissed her forehead. "That's brilliant, so that way, the camp will be protected by the full force of our army." Then he thought while pulling his chin, "Hmm, but what if they need your divine abilities and you're not here?"

"I have anointed my women with the same abilities. Plus, the Domarians have been training the women and me in their style of combat. Also, I have performed a special ceremony of prayers and offering to our goddess. She revealed to me in a dream that she will grant our soldiers favor in their combat effectiveness. That favor will only last three days; then the soldiers will have to make due until we return."

"Hm-mah!" Gangus smacked a long wet kiss on Brehira's cheek. "Brilliant, My Lady. I'll go and tell the men my decision." Then Gangus rushed out of the tent.

The men hated the plan.

They didn't like the idea of only the four of them facing whatever was out there without them. And Dinary argued even harder for his mother not to go, no matter what gifts the goddess had bestowed upon her. Dinary argued to almost disrespect of his father until Brehira stormed out of her tent and smacked Dinary hard across his face and demanded that he apologize to Gangus. Then she walked Dinary away and took him aside. Her eyes burned into his.

"I'm sorry, Mother. You were right to pull me away. The last thing I'd want is to hit my father. But I was just so angry."

"You fool. I wasn't protecting your father. I was protecting you. You don't know him as I do. You didn't see his jaw tightened, I did. If you had struck your father, he would have tied you into so many knots, you would have needed every healing gift I possess to repair you. Now go to your tent!"

"Yes, Mother."

On the third day, the Goblins, this time, were escorted by the Volarian soldiers into the camp. Gangus told them that he would not apologize for killing the Drake but that they would destroy as many of their enemies as they could. The Goblins seemed pleased and gave them a map of the areas they wanted to be cleaned out. There were three areas: a nest overflowing with serpents; hundreds of feline creatures Goblins swore they spotted in the area; and a cave of flying lizards. All of these creatures, once snacks for the Drake— were now troublesome to the Goblins. The Goblins thank them in advance and left the camp.

"I still don't trust them, Lord Abram."

"Neither do I, Celio. They're up to something, and whatever it is, we're not going to know it by staying in camp. They don't know it'll only be the four of us."

"Imagine their surprise if they should come here, thinking we're all out there," Lygone said with a chuckle.

Nazi lean over to Gangus and whispered. "The women are in excellent hands. You know I had a time convincing the Domarians that Shea was Conte's wife. They wouldn't let him into his tent where his wife was sleeping." Gangus chuckled loudly. Nazi continued. "I walked up, and one had the poor man by the throat with one hand, holding him a foot off the ground. And Conte is not a small lad." Gangus continued to chuckle and slapped his knee. "I love those Domarians. We're lucky to have them," Gangus said.

"They need to be tamed, if you ask me," one of the soldiers snapped.

"Are *you* going to do it?" Gangus said raising an eyebrow at him.

The soldier held up his hands and shook his head. "But I don't mind fighting beside them; I tell you that."

The next morning, the foursome set out to clean out the areas the Goblins had marked on the map. There was always the stench of rotting corpses in the Badlands, but none as great as the stench coming from the two-headed snake's nest located in a man size hole in the ground.

"They don't expect us to go down there?" Brehira said making a face at it.

"Oh wait, that's not the entrance," Gangus said. "It was a smudge on the map. Here…over here."

"But, there's nothing threatening in there. Are you sure you're reading the map correctly?"

"Brehira, I brought almost a thousand people over treacherous waters. I think I can read a map."

"All right, you lovebirds," Celio teased.

Gangus scratched his head. "But I don't understand."

"Perhaps you'll understand this," a husky voice said from behind. Startled, the foursome turned just as Gangus' staff and Dinary's sword was ripped from their hands and landed at the feet of an old witch. But the attempt to rip Celio's sword and shield from him failed. She squealed like a pig when her magic bolt bounced off of Celio's shield and shot back to her. Her eyes narrowed, and she gritted her teeth at the appearance of her hand. It had swollen twice its size and covered with purple blisters. Celio flashed a wide grin, and with his sword and shield raised, he attempted to attack the witch, but as he stepped forward, preparing to advance, the witch waved her good hand and immobilized the foursome from the neck down.

Gangus called for his staff, but it did not return. "What did you do to it?"

She laughed hideously and picked up the staff. The Witch had power over the staff but not Celio's sword and shield because of its holy divine nature which is dangerous to evil being such as her.

Dinary tried to move. "You bloody rats!"

"Goblins, you're making a big mistake," Gangus warned.

"Oh, I never told you my name," the goblin said. "It's Hun Grugal."

"Is the name supposed to mean something to us? Because it doesn't." Celio snapped.

"No. Just thought you'd like to know who planned you and your people's demise." He threw his head back and coughed a sinister laugh that chilled Brehira to her bones.

Gangus struggled to move his body but found the strain painful. "If we're not back by nightfall, this place will run black with goblin blood."

"Don't you mean in three days?" Grugal said, holding up three fingers.

He lifted his head towards a tree branch. A dark flying insect, with green eyes almost as big as its head, flew over and landed on his shoulder and said in a squeaking voice, *"We performed a special ceremony of prayers and offering to our goddess."* Then it chirped and said, *"Our soldiers granted favor enhances their combat effectiveness. Chirp! That favor only last three days. Chirp! Soldiers have to make due til we return. Churp!"*

Grugal kissed its mouth and flashed a rotting tooth smile. "One of my many little spies. Isn't he cute? Tasty too." He shoved the insect into his mouth and crunched down. Yellow bile streamed from the side of his mouth. Then he gulped it down and made a yummy sound.

"You're disgusting," Brehira barked. "Free us from this sorcery. We came here to do you a favor, and this is the way you treat us."

"What favor?" Grugal snapped. "We need no favors from the likes of you. What we want, we take. We don't care if the Drake is gone or if it had stayed. Thanks to you, more people will be coming through here. And there'll be more stuff to steal."

"But, what do you want? Whatever we have, we will share," Gangus said trying to reason.

"Share?" The old witch and Grugal laughed. "We don't share...we take," Grugal snapped.

The old witch spoke. "We're going to leave you here, and after three days, the Goblins, along with dark warriors will go in and destroy your people and take your goods. And as for you, soon the night creatures will be wandering by this area. They will attack you where you stand, helpless and alive feeling every tear of your warm flesh as they slowly eat you." She threw her head back and laughed.

"Nighty night," she said turning her back and walking off with Grugal. They disappeared through the thick of the forest. Gangus murmured in despair.

"Father, now don't go thinking this is your fault. It was a great idea. I mean, who could have foreseen this. We're in a land of magic and strange creatures. It's going to take time to learn how to outfox them."

"Nice try, Dinary," Gangus said. "But you told me they couldn't be trusted. And I didn't listen. Maybe I'm getting too old to lead."

"Stop that talk," Dinary said. "I don't want to hear it. Great people make mistakes. And you're the greatest leader I know."

Brehira smiled. "Well, that was sweet. Now that father and son are on speaking terms again. How about, if we high-tale it out of here?" She closed her eyes and said a short prayer then she started grunting and slowly moving until she broke free of the enchantment. "Now, you do the same," she said to them.

"But we don't know what to say," Gangus said bewildered.

"You don't have to; I've done the hard part. You just move."

Gangus and Celio strained and grunted. Finally, Gangus broke free of the magic then Dinary. Celio strained so hard that he landed face down in the dirt at Brehira's feet. She just stood with her hands on her hips and shook her head at him

"What! I'm free," he said looking up at her. Gangus stared at her. "What else did that goddess give you?"

"Let's go see," she said walking away.

Celio jumped up off the ground, and he, Dinary and Gangus followed her. They ran in the direction of the old witch and Grugal to find them and get back their weapons. It seemed like they were walking in circles until Dinary finally found something and ran back to tell the others.

"Over here," he said.

They kept asking what it was until Dinary shushed them and pointed. It was a trap door. They opened and looked down a spiraling stone stairway that was deep and dark, like a bottomless pit and it led into the Goblins' dwelling. Tipping down the stairs took forever. It became darker and darker then a light shone up ahead in a long hallway. Brehira took the lead. They could hear laughing and talking sounds from afar. They continued to tip ever so close until every Goblin sound became magnified. Brehira took a quick peek around into a doorway and saw the staff leaning against the wall. Two Goblins were play-fighting with Dinary's sword. The old hag squinted and peered around the room like she sensed something. "I smell intruders," the old hag said, raising her pointy chin. She sniffed the air like a predator would for prey.

Brehira whispered. "Celio, you get in there and make a ruckus; Dinary, I'll keep the witch busy so you can recover your weapons; Gangus, you grab the staff. "Go." She said. Celio bolted through the doorway and immediately began pummeling several Goblins with his shield and beheading others with his sword. Brehira rushed in chanting a prayer that put a divine shroud of protection around her. Gangus grabbed the staff. He swung the staff, and the wind blew layers of the earth roof off the Goblins' underground home–killing Goblins as the wind smashed them into trees and rocks. Dinary recovered his weapons. His necklace glowed as he joined Celio in decapitating as many Goblins that scrambled into their path.

"Brehira!" Gangus shout, "quickly, behind you."

Brehira shot around and saw ten, twenty, thirty Wraiths rising from the dirt floor. There were no limbs beneath the dirty-grayish robes that they wore. Shadows of their hideous faces sat back, hidden deep within their dark hoods, and their eyes were ablaze. Brehira held out her hand, and wherever they rose from, she rendered them into black dust but still more came.

The witch stared at Brehira's powers in disbelief. She held up her hands and lifted Brehira off her feet and drove her into a wall. But Celio moved up behind her—touched her with his shield. As she jerked violently from the shock, Dinary beheaded her. The death of the witch broke the spell, and the Wraiths disappeared.

The wind from the staff died out, but the surviving Goblins had fled.

When the four stumbled back into camp, they found that the Goblins had not attacked, and everyone was surprised to see them back so quickly. They told them what had happened, and how they had escaped the Goblin's trap. The Domarians wanted to go back and wipe them all out. But Gangus knew that with the witch dead and powers from the gods on their side, the Goblins were no longer a threat.

*****

Fourteen days and eleven hours of travel, and they had finally completed their journey. It was beautiful, and everything Gangus had promised. The land was green as far as the eye could see. There were blue lakes, and green and orange-leaf trees and colorful wild flowers spread throughout the land like the gardens of the gods. There were beautiful, yet, odd creatures: bright yellow and white lizard-like ones flew over the land—some rested on tree branches, and little fuzzy purple creatures with big yellow eyes scurried about the ground. The Volarians stood crying and hugging one another. The soldiers who had died fighting against the ghost ship and the Drake would have their names and rank carved in stones telling for generations their sacrifice.

"You did it, love," Brehira whispered to Gangus, tears rolling down her cheek. "I always believed in you."

Gangus, his own eyes glassy, hugged her close and planted a kiss upon her head.

Chapter Fourteen

Visions of the Gods

Gangus, asleep in his tent—his first night since stepping upon the land that the gods had given him and his people, heard a voice that sounded like a mighty rushing wind. The voice carried him into a vision where he stood before a magnificent figure. Gangus saw that the glory of the figure filled the vast expansion like an endless sea of glass, bright as crystal. Rivers of colorful light appeared as inverted sapphires and flowed from a throne. When Gangus swept his eyes upward and gazed upon the figure, he fell at the foot of the throne as if he were dead.

*****

Earlier in eternity in Zunus—The Realm of Light, a meeting of the gods had taken place. At a round, white, stone table, Raziel, the self-appointed head god, and Gailzur, the God of war, sat waiting on Dahlia. They wore robes that glittered like the stars. "Well, Raziel, they finally made it. What is next?" Gailzur asked.

Raziel spoke matter-of-factly, "Give them time. The Nordoxz will soon venture more to the east where they will come too near Lord Abram and his people. Unlike the other races, once Abram senses the threat, he will build a larger army and fight back.

Gailzur, who wasn't particularly respected by the other gods due to his apparent thirst for bloodshed, laid a finger upon his chin. "Yes, I do recall sometime back when he trained an army of farmers and defeated the Trolls and Ogres—the same Trolls and Ogres, by-the-way, that nearly wiped out the king's armies." Gailzur sat a few more moments fidgeting in his chair, and then muttered, "Where is she?" At that moment, Dahlia made her grand entrance draped in a floor-length, ice-blue, shimmering garment which had a long train. She strolled towards them like she was the queen goddesses.

"Well, it's about time, don't you think?" Gailzur greeted.

She held her train and walked around to each one lifting her cheek for a kiss which they bestowed. "This has better be good. I was just in the middle of elevating twelve, new priestess when you summoned me." She took her seat across from them.

Gailzur cocked his head and made a pity sound with his teeth. "Oh…did we take you away from your little dolls?" He hated the way she doted on, what he called, her six-foot doll babies—and the way she'd taught them not to trust in men.

"Stop calling them that," she snapped.

"Dolls, dolls, silly big dolls," Gailzur repeated annoyingly.

"You call them dolls again and so help me …"

"All right you two," Raziel warned. "We're here to discuss a mortal war, not to start one among the gods." He turned from them momentarily. "I swear you two can't be in the same atmosphere with each other."

Still reeling from Gailzur's comments, she pointed her finger at him but glared at Raziel. "You tell him to stop referring to my dolls; I mean women—"

Gailzur laughed uncontrollably.

"You see, he's gotten me so upset." Then she turned to Gailzur and smirked. "I think I'll send a lightning bolt in the midst of your little tin soldiers you're always playing with."

Gailzur cut off his laugh, his gaze burning. "You do, and I'll turn those man-hating rag dolls into eighty-year-old hags. Let's see who'll mate with them then."

"Stop it, both of you," Raziel warned. "I am tired of refereeing you two every time we come together. The Nordoxz are going to destroy Bethica if we don't do something. Now, try to get along!"

"What's the matter," Nelchael, the god of death, spoke from the shadows, "forget how to rain down fire from the sky? Sounds like you're getting soft," Nelchael said with a sinister laugh.

Dahlia turned quickly to where the voice came. Nelchael stood deep within the shadows—his long robe was as black as a moonless night and sparkled like crushed crystal embedded in volcanic rock. "You'd like that wouldn't you, Nelchael?" she scoffed. "You'd like raising more foul creatures from the dead like you did in Horromog and Modes."

"That's right, blame me. Mortals couldn't possibly be evil all by themselves."

"You deny it?"

"Of course I do. The Soul is Powerful, remember? You should know that from the last world we tried to rule. You-know-who and his fallen Ones are the reason why we left."

She gritted her teeth and tightened her fists. "We do not speak of him here!"

Nelchael laughed loudly. "Calm yourself, dear Dahlia. What are you afraid of? He received his just reward, didn't he?"

"Dahlia, Nelchael," Raziel interjected. "I hate to break up this little randevu, but if we could get back to the matter at hand…and to answer your question, Nelchael. Raining down fire would destroy Bethica. We don't want to make the same mistake with this world."

"I have a question."

Raziel was more than happy to answer Gailzur's question and turn from their bickering. "Yes, Gailzur. "

"What do we have for Dinary?"

"I can answer that," Dahlia said fingering with her sparkling bracelets. "Zakzakiel has plans of his own for him—though he hasn't said much. The necklace he gave Dinary is very powerful and, I believe, will be instrumental in defeating the Nordoxz."

"Oh, yes," Gailzur said. "I forgot how mysterious Zakzakiel could be. He's always done things his own way. And where is he, anyway?"

Dahlia pulled out a mirror and started primping her hair. "Zakzakiel prefers being among the mortals. I've never understood why. He either walks invisibly among them or in fleshy Incognito." She twisted a curl then put away her mirror.

"Well," Raziel said, speaking loudly to the shadow, so Nelchael knew very well he was speaking about him, "at least he's on our side and not making the Nordoxz in the west a growing threat and using black magic to create beasts to do their bidding."

"Hmm, sounds like something I would do. But sorry…wrong again. You know, it's amazing how you three can play chest moves with the lives of your subjects. And with a straight face no doubt." Nelchael laughed deeply and loudly, with the sound of his laughter trailing off into silence.

"Good, he's gone," Raziel spoke further with anger trembling in his voice. "Now do you see why it's important for Lord Gangus Abram to succeed? That's why we are here—to work together to save the Land of Bethica from the Nordoxz."

"I suspect Nelchael too, though I have no proof. But why do you keep insisting that I have men worship me? Why can't I just send my warriors to fight with Gangus? I've given his wife Brehira more than I've given any woman. Why can't that be enough?" She sat back and shook her head in disgust.

Gailzur leaned forward and spoke quietly to her. "Because it will take team worship to bring down the Nordoxz, and your women won't worship anyone but you. And you've encouraged them not to take orders from men. And most importantly, my dear Dahlia, you have gifts our male priest and warriors could use to build a powerful fighting force."

"Dahlia," Razil pleaded, "don't you see unless we can bestow all of our gifts on one army and have full worship and loyalty from all of our servants… including priest and priestess, we cannot hope to destroy the powerful and undefeated Nordoxz. Every army Gailzur and I have inspired, went down defeated by untrained, incompetent or cowardly men who turned and fled. We need Gangus, who can train men to be fearless."

"But before he can do that," Gailzur interjected. "…he must raise a mighty army from among the Timbakni, Engamars, Aenwyns, and Qu'Venars. It won't be easy since they always resist getting involved in anything that doesn't directly threaten them. Plus, they don't particularly trust each other," he continued. "But I believe he *is* the only man who could pull them together."

"Yes, it is true," she said, placing a finger against her cheek. "He does show great promise. No mortal has ever killed a Drake or fought against the undead the way he and his men fought. And Raziel…he has never failed you." She thought awhile, then said, "All right, I'll instruct Brehira to choose priest from among her male people. Besides, Gangus' staff will have little effect on the Nordoxz with their strong resistance to magic. Only weapons of Divine nature can destroy *that* evil. "

Raziel blew out a breath of relief, "Finally, my dear Dahlia, you have come to understand this."

Surprised at her sudden change of heart, Gailzur looked upon her kindly. "I apologize, for all the times I spoke harshly of your priestess." He smiled and held out his hand. "Shall we call a truce?" She took his hand and cupped it within hers. "All I ever wanted was your respect, Gailzur, and you have shown it."

Gangus trembled in a cold sweat as he laid face-down at the foot of the figure. For no mortal had ever been summoned to the throne of Raziel.

"Rise, Lord Abram. You are not dreaming, and this is not my natural form; that is forbidden to every mortal. You've received a great gift. For to other mortals, I am but a voice, but to you, my loyal servant, I have brought you to stand before me."

Gangus stood shaking in his night clothes. "B…but, w…where am I?"

"When you are in my presence, you are everywhere, and you are nowhere. I am Raziel, the god of gods. I have brought you here to say that I am pleased with you. You have made the journey. And throughout your quest, I will be with you and will never leave you. I have set you far above my other subjects, and will not tolerate any disobedience from you. Is that clear?"

"Yes, Great Lord, as you wish." Gangus snapped awake, and he was back in his bed with Brehira sleeping soundly beside him. He jumped up and went to where he hid his staff. It was still there, and beside it, two two-edged steel swords. There was no shield, but a breast plate made of a shiny, blue metal. On the front was the symbol of Raziel. Gangus stepped back from his gifts and put a hand over his heart. He again received something of a Divine nature, not from an oracle, but from Raziel, himself, the god of gods. Gangus could finally put an image with the voice. And even though the image was not the true likeness of Raziel, Gangus was, nonetheless, still pleased.

Chapter Fifteen

Engamars

One morning while a group of Volarian settlers was mining on the outskirts of a mountain, armed creatures known as Engamars approached them with weapons drawn. The Volarians were startled by the Engamars who were short and stout with red hair and beards. More surprising were the females whose red beards were much shorter than the males', and they wore fitted attire that came to their ankles and leather boots up to their knees. The Engamars carried the typical iron swords and shields, with metal greaves to protect their shins and wore metal head gear with an iron spike right in the middle. The Engamars reluctantly allowed the settlers to leave without incident, but threatened and warned them never to mine there again. When the near fatal incident reached the ear of Gangus, he hurried to the Engamar leader bearing gifts of wine.

After the leader had tasted the wine, he became very apologetic for mistaking the miners for thieves, but as far as allowing them to mine near Engamar Mountains, he said gruffly, "I'll have to give it a little more thought." Week after week for several months, the Engamar leader insisted on giving the matter a little more thought—usually after a few sips of this new drink called wine. And still every week dutifully, Gangus approved more wine to be sent, hoping to change the leader's mind. Finally, after much thought, and wine, Gangus was sent their approval to mine. The settlers were ecstatic, and thus began a long friendship between the two races. Of course, the settlers never knew that the Engamars had readily agreed among themselves months ago to allow settlers to mine, but never told them. The Engamars had noticed that every time they didn't agree, the settlers would send more wine to entice them. So, they decided to drag their feet until they were able to store as many goat skins of wine as they could. This little deceit was quite unusual for the mountain dwellers that were known as creatures of honor and high reputation. But thanks to the Volarians, the Engamars had grabbed a little piece of heaven for themselves by being the first of their realm to add *wine* to women and song.

*****

Warren W. Randall, Jr.

Though living near the Volarian army offered great protection, many settlers weren't content with living in a village. They'd had enough of small village life and wanted to build their homes and farms out in the open—far from neighbors; and so, they left Gangus and ventured out into the wilderness to build upon a piece of land. Doing this, however, took great risk, and it came back to haunt many of them.   A group of men headed out into the forest as they usually did around a certain time of day, but unlike the days before, they didn't return for their evening meal, and their wives worried. When nightfall came, and they still had not returned, a few of their wives waited until morning then climbed into wagons and rode into the settlement to plead to Celio to find them. A small troupe of swordsmen was immediately sent to escort them back and to search the forest for their men. But after night fell, they also did not return.

Gangus remembered the Engamars and sent Olutunji alone bearing gifts of grapes, potatoes, onions, spices and of course, wine. As Olutunji searched through the thickness of the forest, he spotted evidence of a scuffle and freshly cut tree stumps. Suddenly, a small puff of wind whizzed past his ear, and he heard a thump. He turned and gasped when he saw an arrow sticking into a tree trunk just inches from his head which made him stumble back. Several female Aenwyns stood with their bows drawn.

Olutunji threw up his hands, dropping the gifts. "I come in peace," he said. They stood like statues with eyes partially hidden behind their bows. "See, I bear gifts." He bent down, picked up the sack from the end and dumped the vegetables on the ground. "Po ta toes," he said slowly pronouncing each syllable. They muttered among themselves in their language. He held up an onion and a bunch of grapes, "Un yuns...gray apes." The wine he kept for the leader, he popped a few grapes into his mouth and held out several in his hands, moving slowly towards them—every arrow pointing at his head. He exaggerated chewing and made a yummy sound. But they appeared to ignore his delight. With their bows still drawn, they spoke harshly to him in their language. Though he didn't understand, he did figure out from the glare in their eyes, and their drawn bows that he was going with them whether he wanted to or not.

After moments of being captured, Olutunji finally discovered what had happened to the woodsmen and his fellow soldiers when the Aenwyns took his sack and placed him in lockup with them, but in a separate cell. Each shared their experiences with being captured, and after a long stretch of time, only Olutunji was allowed from his cell after Gangus came to talk to one of the leader. Gangus told him that Olutunji had grown the vegetables that his soldiers had confiscated. It so happened that the Aenwyns were master farmers, and were very well taken with Olutunji's knowledge. The Aenwyns Princes told Gangus that the woodsmen and soldiers were allowed to leave and agreed they could use the Aenwyns' forest for their lumber. Though the Aenwyns preferred to deal with Olutunji because of their shared knowledge and love of the land, the respect between them made it possible for trade among the Volarians and the Aenwyns that led to a lasting friendship.

*****

Thirty-seven years passed with peaceful living among the indigenous people of the new land. Gangus and his people knew much prosperity. There were vast lands of animal and vegetable farms, fruit trees and grape vines. There were mills, a town hall, bakeries, clothing shops, schools, and temples, just to name a few. Lord and Lady Abram lived in a magnificent manor house, surrounded by other mansions that were built for Volarians of note. And many small colorful houses were scattered throughout the villages.

A stone wall with a round tower facing in every direction was both defense and decoration. The guards kept the vaulted gate closed at night. Though over the years, there were many small skirmishes against intruders who tried and failed to invade the land, the people never regretted following Gangus to the new world. The Volarians quickly acquired a reputation as a people best not to make as an enemy. But though their reputation had kept some invaders at bay—this newest breed didn't seem to care.

Dinary became general of his men—now called, the Guards with Celio second in command. Nazi, Kofius, Olutunji, and Lygone each commanded their own regiments. General Dinary and his wife Princess Lerayah had two sons: Rahshi, the oldest, and Glinas. Rahshi and Glinas joined the Guards and served under Celio in a small 40-man unit, called The Blue Dragon, named by their defeated enemies because of their blue breast plates and because of the ruthless way they fought. The unit was responsible for spotting and attacking invaders before they ventured too close to the outskirts of Volarian land. Rahshi was an expert archer and Glinas, taught by Gangus, fought with two double-edged swords. Rahshi married first and had three daughters. Then Glinas married Lurah and later, Rahkia who both bore him many sons. Gangus and Brehira, proud grandparents, were in charge of preparing their great grandsons to be rulers of their future empires.

*****

"Commander, sir," Glinas said addressing Celio. "We just wiped out another band not far from the lake." Celio took his time looking up from the map he was studying. It was used to keep track of the invaders and took up nearly half the six-foot table. On the map were tiny shapes like chess figures. And each figure appeared to be placed closer and closer to the settlement.

"Is that your blood or theirs?" he said calmly, sweeping his eyes over Glinas. These little skirmishes were ongoing and of no surprise to Celio which was the reason for his serenity.

Glinas looked down at the blood smear. "I believe it's theirs', sir."

"You need to go to the Medicus just the same," Celio said. He turned his attention back to the map. But then he noticed that Glinas didn't move, and he inquired if there was something more he needed to say. Glinas hesitated then told him that there was something different about these invaders. He said they were well trained and fought like the very devil. He said that their armor didn't look to be from around this area. And after they had killed them, they found lots of coins. Celio didn't like the sound of that. Every time he'd heard anything about the invaders nearby, he was careful to note on the map where the incident took place. He couldn't believe that someone in this area had that amount of coins to pay mercenaries to do their dirty deeds. Then Glinas told him something further that gave Celio few doubts that this was the work of a well-organized leader. Glinas said one of the men laughed and muttered that a storm was coming. He said it over and over—laughing until he died. "I kept asking him what it meant. But he just laughed and said death was coming for us all."

Celio's calm demeanor quickly turned to panic as he rushed from his quarters and told one of the guards to have General Dinary, the commanders, all captains, and The Blue Dragons to meet him at Lord and Lady Abrams immediately. After all had assembled, Celio had Glinas to repeat everything he'd told him. The room fell deathly silent.

*****

Several months passed without incident or a single report concerning possible mercenaries. Rumors about the exact identities of intruders were always accurate due to the distinct characteristics of all the races in Bethica. Celio scratched his beard and stared at the map—wondering what the settlers would be up against next. He thought ahead and had some ideas, but didn't want to alarm the others with his concerns, because he had no facts to back them up. He simply had to wait, he thought, for them to make another move.

And they did.

"Open the gate!" a guard shouted from the tower.

A middle-aged man, blood streaming down his face stumbled into the settlement's gate with his foot nearly severed. He managed to walk the long distance with nothing but a long, thick tree branch to hold him up. The minute the guards grabbed him, he fell exhausted into their arms. "My wife, my boys," the man said straining his voice through a screwed face.

"Who did this, Cresley?" another guard asked.

The battered man looked up at the guards—his face in a cry with no sound coming from it. "I tried to save them. I tried to save them."

"You tried to save them from whom? Speak up, man."

"They…they were Orc-like…strange skin," he muttered through blood-dripping lips."

"How many?"

"Twenty… maybe thirty," he grunted, and then closed his eyes and went limp.

"Get him over to the healers," the head guard said. "I'll report this to Celio."

Many settlers had continued to respectfully reject Gangus' advice about moving too far west near where attacks were taking place. After Celio had been alerted, he had the injured man questioned after he'd been treated by the healers and was fully conscious. Celio learned there were strange spotted creatures in that area for weeks, but not reported. Nearly a hundred settlers had been axed to death—whole families at a time. Cresley said that when he had run one through with his sword, the creature had this horrible look of surprise before he died—as if he'd never felt the pain of steel before. After that, they took his sword and tortured him when he failed to reveal the mystery of the Volarian-made metal. Then they forced him to watch his wife, and three sons cut to pieces right before his eyes. He tried to save them, but he was cut down and left for dead. With a deep gash in his skull and a mangled foot, he had traveled through the night—leaking a trail of blood before reaching the settlement.

A small group was sent out to spy the land and to access the damages. When they returned, they reported to Celio, and he reported to Dinary. It was the first time the settlers heard the name Nordoxz.

"Father, I don't think these were mercenaries this time." He had to use two hands to lift the sword and place it on the table in front of Gangus. The heavy blade, though inferior, was well made and had rare stones embedded in the handle. "The settlers managed to kill only a few of them. I questioned a few Engamars about the incident, and they mentioned they were Nordoxz hell-bent on finding out about our steel. I can't understand why they never mentioned this to us."

Gangus looked up from the blade and smoothed his hand down his white beard. "Creatures in this realm are very strange. No matter how friendly they are, they seem undisturbed by other races' dilemmas. I warned the settlers that moving so far out would make it impossible for our troops to protect them. Don't know why they're so fascinated with moving so far west."

Brehira stepped behind Gangus and placed a soothing hand on his shoulder. "The land is so green, rich and inviting; I guess it's just too hard for them to say no to it when it calls them," she reasoned.

"I can understand them wanting to get away from village life having lived that way all their lives in the old world," Gangus said, patting her hand. "But, it's not worth falling into the beastly hands of such enemies. Gangus fingered his white beard and wondered who these spotted creatures were and when they'd strike next.

Chapter Sixteen

Clash of the Orcs

Gangus was a wise man but could also rely heavily on that sick feeling he'd get whenever bad things were soon to happen. Brehira called it a warning from the gods. But whatever it was, Gangus saw it manifest into the many skirmishes they had with the Goblinoid races, such as 'Goblins, HobGoblins, and Bugbears.' To put Gangus' mind at ease, Dinary ordered Celio and an advance guard of twenty men to scout out the far west into Nordoxz territory; they were to find out as much as they could about these spotted creatures that struck such fear, that the name, Nordoxz had to be whispered.

One fact Celio quickly discovered was that before he and his men could get near the Nordoxz, they had to get past their Orc allies. After the Nordoxz had given a show of might and a promise of wealth, the Orcs agreed to fight for the Nordoxz and to kill anyone who ventured too far into the western territory. And true to life, once inside the region of the west, the Orcs attacked them. But with their superior blades of steel, the guards made short work of the Orcs, cutting them down and leaving their bodies on the open road for scavengers. However, many days later, after the guards had set up camp, fifty Orcs attacked them as they slept. This incident devastated Celio; the attack left him with only nine soldiers who were severely cut and bruised but would survive thanks to his divine gift of healing.

Weeks later, as if an evil god would have it, they also encountered a Cyclops that stood sixteen feet tall. The giant creature killed another four of Celio's men and would have killed them all, had Celio not thrown a spear into its eye. As the giant cried out in pain—stumbling about, it fell on its back kicking as blood gushed from its face. Celio, you could say, mercifully put it out of its misery by whacking off its head, or, perhaps not so merciful—but just wanted to keep the sightless monster's cries from bringing unwanted attention.

Many more days came and went. The men camped, fished and hunted peacefully without incident. Then around midnight, under a dim moonlight, one of the soldiers got up to relieve himself and spotted a blaze of fire from a short distance away. He woke Celio who quickly gathered the men to go, spy. Crawling on their bellies, they hopped to their feet and scurried behind some bushes. They spotted well over twenty Orcs sitting around a fire drinking something from a small bowl. But what was most astonishing was right behind them were cages of creatures that appeared to have feline-like features. Unconcerned, Celio turned to leave when something caught his eye that made him squint to get a better look. He gasped when he saw some of the settlers, his people, in cages next to the feline creatures. "Good goddess, those are our men," he whispered pointing.

The men became enraged and pulled their swords, but Celio's raised hand stopped them. Celio reasoned that there stood only him and four guards to face nearly thirty Orcs. He decided that one of them would sneak around to the back and unlock the settler's cage. Celio knew his colonists would fight but wasn't too sure of the creatures. Perhaps, they'd just run away. As long as they stayed out of their way, Celio could have cared less.

The men waited patiently for the Orcs to bed down for the night. Whatever was in those small bowls they were slurping up, had them sleeping like babies. Celio could swear their snoring was heard for miles.

One of the men, tall with a dark complexion like Olutunji, who could blend well with the night, crept unnoticed within the camp as the Orcs dribbled all over themselves, while others made strange noises out of the holes in their faces. One of the settlers' spotted him, and the soldier put his finger up to his lips for him not to make a sound. He inched closer to the cage crawling on his belly—one of the feline creatures stirred and lifted its head from an old sack used as a pillow, but froze when he saw the soldier unlock the settler's cage door. One by one, the settlers tipped from the cage. With half of them out, the remaining ones froze with fear when an Orc stirred. Their hearts pounded in their chest while the Orc snorted loudly, scratched his butt and turned over on his side. Then they breathed freely when the stirring Orc fell once again into deep sleep. The remaining few tipped out of the cage and joined the others who led the soldier to where they kept additional weapons. Some settlers grabbed up the few bows and arrows; others were disappointed to have to use the inferior iron blades. The soldier signaled Celio and the guards an "all is well" sign. A few feline creatures made gestures for the soldier to let them out. But the soldier shook his head.

"We can help you," one said in a loud whisper.

The soldier shook his head again and tried to focus his attention on the soon-to-be-battle.

"Please, let us out," the same creature begged.

"Quiet," the soldier ordered in a loud whisper. "You'll just be in the way. We won't leave you behind. I promise."

"But we can fight," said the same creature.

"No," the soldier whispered. "And besides, there are no more weapons."

All of the feline creatures were now upon their feet; when the soldier attempted to ease past their cage, they shot out two-inch claws and drew back their lips to display their needle-point fangs.

"Will these do?" the feline creature asked.

The soldier's eyes flash wide, and a slow grin etched across his face. He nodded, tipped to the side of the cage—peeked around, then stretched his arm and unhooked the lock on the cage. When Celio and the guards met the soldier at the rear of the camp, he told Celio that the feline creatures wanted to fight. Celio welcomed the creatures with a nod and a smile. And as the Orcs appeared to battle each other to which could snore the loudest, the guards, settlers and feline creatures bent low while Celio whispered a plan.

After the scheme was well understood, the first thing Celio did was to bid his fellow settlers to get rid of those iron swords, and he replaced them with ones that belonged to his fallen guards. The feline creatures were to return to their cage and pretend to be locked in. Celio, the guards, and settlers were only twelve strong; this made them well out-numbered by the Orcs. The plan was to kill as many Orcs as they could while they slept then make the remaining Orcs chase them throughout the camp. During the organized confusion, the seventeen feline creatures would emerge in a full surprise attack and aid the Volarians.

Celio's and his men crept upon the sleeping creatures with their blades and quietly slit their throats. One tough old Orc defied death and fought off his attacker, but eventually fell dead at the settler's feet. The noise woke an Orc who jumped from his bedding with a sword in his hand and shouted, "We're under attack!" The loud cry woke the Orcs who jumped to their feet—their eyes bulging, and peering around for their weapons; they confronted the Volarian band. But instead of fighting—true to plan, the group took off running, and the chase was on. Around the camp and off through the woods, the men ran with the Orcs lagging behind. The band of men laughed as they toyed with the Orcs who were tall, bulky and slow which made it hard for them to keep up with the smaller Volarians. The band continued taunting the Orcs: making the creatures chase them through the woods and around trees, forcing them to stumble over huge rocks, swiping and missing the Volarians then landing face down with their mouths full of dirt.

Back at the camp, Celio stood over five Orcs he had cut down with his divine blade, but a sixth one ran into a nearby cave yelling. Celio reckoned the creature was summoning more of its comrades. When the Orc ran out, Celio cut him down and entered the cave ready to face the Orcs, but instead, Celio froze with his mouth gaped.

Frustrated with the soldiers and settlers toying with them, the Orcs finally cornered the men who were out of breath. The Orcs moved in to strike when the feline creatures leaped upon the Orcs, tearing into them with their sharp claws and deadly fangs with the settlers joining in. The bloodbath was over in minutes. As the settlers and the feline creatures stood rejoicing over the spread of Orc bodies upon the ground, Celio stumbled into camp, cut and bleeding, his sword faintly glowing green and dripping with a black substance.

"Commander, what happened?"

"It's...it's in the cave," Celio said out of breath.

A few of the men ran to the cave; they stood with their eyes bulging. It was a huge, dark creature unknown to Volarians, called a Minotaur, that was lying eight feet in length and muscular. It had the head of a bull and the body of a man. The bullhead was laying several inches from its body. They returned to camp and told the others of their find.

Celio had to rely on the Medicus because he had used up his divine power for the day fighting the Minotaur; so, nothing remained for healing. While Celio sat having his wounds bandaged, a settler noticed movement. An Orc was trying to escape. "Look there!" the settler yelled pointing.

"After him!" shouted Morkii, the second in command.

Two guards bolted, when a settler yelled, "I've got him." The men skid to a halt as the settler aimed his bow at the Orc's back

But Celio said, "No! Raco, see where he goes. Leave markings so we can find you."

"Yes, Commander." Raco ran off into the forest where the darkness swallowed him up.

Celio felt the weight of the battle; he was exhausted. His divine blade had taken out three Orcs at a time. His men and settlers stood above him breathing hard with sweat rolling off of them like pearls. The feline people, who fought gallantly, were hardly out of breath and complained that the fight was over too soon. The blood covered the camp ground. Heads and other body parts of Orcs lay in the midst of it. Having no time to embrace one another before the fight, the settlers grabbed and hugged the guards. They hugged Celio as well; then Celio turned to thank the feline creatures who introduced themselves as Nekani—a furry race of feline humanoids with green, yellow and sometimes gray eyes. They were a highly civilized race who was third in the grand exodus from the west to Bethica generations ago. The Nekanies were great warriors. Nekanies did not fear death; they courted it like you would a lover. They wrote songs and poems about death. They were known as creatures who strived for a good death, which meant to fall in combat.

The spokesman for the Nekani was Tantar, a tall, muscular humanoid with solid tan fur and green eyes. He thanked Celio and his men for releasing him and his clan and told Celio that he would always remember that the Volarians had been kind. "If ever the Nekani can do anything for you or your people in the future," Tantar said, "please grant us that honor."

"I'll deliver your message to my people," Celio assured him.

Tantar and Celio embraced then the Nekanies went on their way. Soon after, Celio gathered the spoils of the Orcs, which included, pouches of metal coins, jewelry of fine stones—taken from the dead bodies, water, meal, herbs, spices and a strange leaf, dark blue with thick red veins spread throughout. He would take the exotic plant back to Olutunji for him to examine and see if it were fit for Volarian consumption or medicinal use. With the spoils packed, all headed for the forest to follow Raco and the fleeing Orc.

*****

Celio and his band had traveled for several days, following Raco's markings which only Volarians hunters understood. They had advanced deep inside of the western territory where things were beginning to look a bit strange: There were fist-size rocks, painted red, lining a path. Humanoid heads draped in ceremonial dressings were nailed to every tree; Celio stopped when he spotted a stagnant pool of yellow water with hundreds of plants like the strange one he had slipped in a pouch back at the Orc and Minotaur camp, floating on top.

Stagnant water meant disease. This plant can't be of any good use, Celio thought, pulling the plant from the pouch and rolling it between his fore finger and thumb. Then he quickly tossed it aside and wiped his hand hard on the side of his garment as he thought it could be poison. Celio started to leave it there, but couldn't resist knowing what it was. He tore a piece of his garment, bent down and covered the plant with the cloth, picked it up and placed it back in the pouch.

"Commander!" Celio didn't like the sound of that urgent cry. "Dear goddess, what now," he whispered. He ran up ahead as fast as he could. When he got there, the ban was surrounding something and looking down. He pushed between two of his guards and discovered Raco's body lying face down with an arrow in his back.

The anger in Celio's face tightened his jaw. "Bloody hell, Raco. I shouldn't have let you go alone," he said kneeling beside Raco's body. Celio lowered his head and exhaled hard. Then he lifted his eyes and saw something sticking out the side of Raco's mouth. Celio grabbed the end of it and pulled. It was a folded cloth, wet with Raco's saliva and blood. Celio unfolded the fabric, and his eyes widened. He bent and kissed Raco on the head.

"What is it, Commander?" Morkii asked.

"A soldier to the bitter end," Celio said half smiling. Celio stood—turning the piece of cloth up-side-down, sideways and straight up again, trying to make out the scribblings on the Raco-made map.

"Here, wash the blood off," Markii said handing him a container of water.

"No. Raco gave his blood to get this map to us. I don't want water to touch it."

"What does it say," asked Prefus, one of the settlers.

Celio turned it sideways and squinted. "It shows the layout of the Orc and Minotaur army camp; and behind them, the Nordoxz."

"Does it say how many there are?" Prefus blurted. "Their strength…their weakness, their weapons?

Celio squinted again—trying to make out Raco's scribblings. "Hundreds of thousands of Orcs, Minotaurs, and Nordoxz; bows, arrows, spears, swords, all made of iron but with poison tips; some strange beasts. He drew the animal here." They all gathered and peeked over Celio's shoulder to get a glimpse of the drawing.

"What's that symbol there?" asked Lympus, one of the guards.

"I don't know," Celio said frowning. "I guess when we see it; we'll know we're there." Celio sighed. "Poor Raco."

"But Commander," Markii urged, "why not just take him home with us. He'll smell for a while. But Lady Abram could still bring him back?"

"I'm afraid not, Markii," Celio said sadly, "by the time we get back, weeks would have passed. Indeed, the gods have blessed us with great gifts, but the resurrection gifts can only work within ten days of death, and it will take us longer than that to return home."

"Oh…I see, Sir," Markii said dropping his head.

Celio ordered the band to bury Raco which took nearly an hour. He wanted him buried deep so no scavengers could dig him up. He and the band knelt by the grave and prayed. With sundown quickly approaching, Celio ordered the group to gather their gear and head back to the settlement.

*****

When Celio and his guards returned home, they were given a hero's welcome for rescuing their fellow settlers and bringing back valuable information for which Raco had risked his life. Gangus, Dinary, including Celio and other commanders, studied the map repeatedly and created strategies for the battle.

According to the eye-account of Raco, the Orcs were about ten legions strong (Thirty thousand men); the Minotaurs, looked to be nine thousand, and the Nordoxz, thirty thousand. Gangus and Dinary calculated that the Volarians would probably have to be at least four to five legions strong. As the men continued to finalize their plans, Brehira was busy helping her student priests and priestess perfect their divine gifts, none, unfortunately, would be ready for the battle that was soon to come.

Six weeks into the planning and the Volarians felt ready. They loaded dry goods, such as figs, dates and unleavened bread onto several ox-pulled carts. They also packed medicinal supplies, binding cloth, goat skins of water and extra weapons. The men would head out under cover of darkness—traveling and sleeping in the open to avoid an ambush.

The women kissed their men tearfully and gave them little items of scarfs, jewelry, tiny statues of Raziel—anything they made as a symbol of the men's safe return.

Filing out of the settlement, Gangus led the way holding his staff like a scepter while General Dinary and Celio road by his side. Weeks of travel, training, and several nights' rest, the Volarian army reached their destination. The Orcs who had stalked them, hiding in the shadows of the thick forest, could have ambushed them at any time but was ordered not to by their Commander.

"They'll die soon enough, the arrogant Minotaur leader," had said, "I'll not have it said we won by cowardly tactics."

The Volarian army stood five legions strong (Ten thousand foot-soldiers and a Calvary of five thousand). Three thousand were left behind to guard the homeland. With Brehira's and her priests and priestess' divine gifts, Gangus felt confident that the homeland would be safe. However, rather or not he and his men would return home in one piece became quite concerning when he finally faced their foe of ten thousand Orcs and a small group of Minotaurs who stood on a high hill and watched. Gangus didn't like the looks of that. He could smell a trick brewing. And he was right. A Minotaur army of nine thousand was camped not far—ready to aid the Orcs in a moment's notice if and when the horn-call sounded. Each battle horn purposely had its unique sound so that each army knew their call.

The Nordoxz and Raco's poorly drawn beast were nowhere in sight. None-the-less, the Volarians were there to wipe out the troublesome Orcs who had been a thorn in their side since they had settled in the region thirty-seven years ago; and if that meant destroying the Minotaurs—then in the hot pits of Hades, they would join their flunky Orcs. Gangus raised his hand, and the battle horn sounded. The thunder of the horse's hooves on both sides of the battle field rose from the ground like a rumbling earth quake, their heads bobbing, noses widening to pull in the air necessary for their long legs to eat up the ground as the steeds met head to head in the middle of the battle field. The tinkling sounds of metal striking metal filled the air as the steel swords of the Volarian army cut in half the inferior iron swords of the Orcs—leaving them weaponless and headless on the battle floor. Arrows flew through the air like wingless birds on both sides, killing Volarians and Orcs the like. Although the iron was no match for steel, the expert archery of the Orcs with its highly poisonous tips kept the battle quite even for many, many months. Plus, Gangus' staff, with limits on the amount of time it could operate throughout the day, was useless against the fast-past ongoing attacks from the Orc army. After the Orcs were nearly wiped out (though, some ran and were never seen in that region again), the Minotaurs disappeared from the hill. Gangus thought that very strange. But he didn't have to wonder very long; after a small victory and a week resting. One morning, a scout bolted into camp shouting that nine thousand Minotaurs were marching within a mile of them. The battle with the Orcs had lasted eleven grueling months, and Gangus had lost three thousand men. With a reserve nearby, Gangus stood once again with five legions including the Calvary. The Minotaur's could fight five at a time; so, their nine thousand was like thirty thousand; but there were still the Volarian's superior swords of steel and mighty archers to make up the difference. In spite of that, the war with the Minotaurs lasted fifteen months, and the stench of dead Minotaurs filled the air. Flesh-eating birds came from far and wide to feast on their massive caucuses.

Days of burying the dead and attending to the wounded, provided Gangus, Dinary and Celio enough time to confer that the Minotaurs never intended to aid the Orcs. It was the Nordoxz all along that both were protecting: If the Orcs couldn't stop them, then the Minotaurs would; and if they couldn't, then the Nordoxz would defend themselves. But where were they?

Dinary sent Lygone back to the midway point to sound the alarm for more reserves. Gangus had lost six thousand. But the mystery was over; again he stood strong with five legions against the mighty Nordoxz of thirty thousand including the strange beasts Raco had poorly drawn. The beasts were the Nordoxz's secret weapon: eight-legged large wolf-like creatures, dark coarse fur, and long snouts. They foamed at the mouth, and the foam was poisonous. They would spit the foam that acted like acid on the toughest hide of their opponents. With their mighty jaws, they could crush bone like chewing wax.

Having never seen such beasts before, the sight of them caused the horses to stir, bobbing their heads and clopping in place. The men talked in their ears and patted their long necks to steady them. But like true and tried horse-soldiers of previous wars, when the battle horn blew, the horses took off like bats soaring from a cave—meeting the Bohaus head-on. Sadly, they were no match for the massive beasts that rammed their legs, breaking them, tearing out their throats and killing their riders. It was the third year of the battle—a bloodbath. Gangus' lost was massive, seven thousand men and five thousand horses. The steel swords just weren't enough to defeat the Nordoxz. Plus the

Nordoxz were able to grab up the steel swords of Gangus' fallen comrades and use them against the Volarians. Gangus had no choice but to order the sound of retreat. The Nordoxz bellowed with laughter as the Volarian army fled in humiliating defeat.

After weeks of traveling, Gangus, Dinary, Celio, and Lygone with their torn and wounded military, dragged across the landscape of their region and into the arms of their loved ones. At least the homeland was still standing.

Sadness spread throughout the settlement, and Gangus wrestled with defeat. He would not stand by and let those spotted creatures take over the land. He had traveled too far: survived the Endless Sea, destroyed cannibal humanoids, fought the undead, and slew a dragon. He was not going to lose what he and his people had worked nearly forty years for. He'd face them again—not alone this time. But how, he thought, could he convince the other races to help? He agonized over many ideas. Finally, Brehira wrote letters to the leaders of the Timbakni, Engamar and Aenwyns races, on Gangus' behave, informing them of the Volarians' dilemma and requesting a meeting. She ended each letter with, Please send a reply. But after several months, they heard nothing.

Chapter Seventeen

The Great Conference

Gangus had returned home from a month long trip and immediately met with his generals to discuss battle strategy and the best way to defend their borders. They went over the numbers repeatedly for weeks, and the problem remained the same: They lacked the body count needed to repel the Nordoxz indefinitely. Plus, the war dogs made a cavalry charge impossible; even steel arrows didn't sink deep enough into their tough hides to damage organs. A sword or spear in the eyes dropped them quickly enough, but roaring up behind them would be the Nordoxz, whose skills with a blade more than matched the best of his soldiers. Gangus sat engulfed with his thoughts—his head pounding in disappointment when Brehira came running with four letters bearing royal seals. She entered Gangus' study with a thud which made Gangus nearly jump out of his skin.

"Brehira, for god's sake, you trying to give me a heart attack?"

Brehira was panting with excitement. "Here," she said, handing Gangus the letters.

"Honey, sit down. You know you're not as young as you use to be," he teased.

"Oh, shut up and open them before I pinch your nose."

Gangus chuckled then looked at one of the seals. "Um, I've never seen this seal before. I better open this one last. He broke the seal of the Timbakni and was delighted to hear from his old friend, Priest Hayman. Gangus read the letter to Brehira. He would attend the meeting and have expressed his honor at long last to assist Gangus any way he could. "Any foe of yours is a foe of the Timbakni," he wrote.

"Ah, I knew the Priest wouldn't let us down," Brehira said smiling widely. "Well, come on, come on."

"All right, I'm opening it," Gangus said fumbling to break the royal seal of the Engamars. He read King Pyruss' words to Brehira who grinned uncontrollably. And they both chuckled when the King ended with a little hint of an attack of a dry cough and how a bit of wine at the meeting could help. After thirty-seven years, the Engamars had learned the art of wine making, but the recipe had been in Abram's family for many generations and that perfection had been missing from King's Pyruss' taste buds.

The sound of the third seal snapping made both their hearts race. It was the royal seal of the Aenwyns. The Aenwyns had a powerful army. The corners of Brehira's mouth turned down when she watched deep lines inch across Gangus' forehead.

"Well, what does King Lakni say, Love?"

"No."

"NO?" She pulled the letter from his hand and read the explanation. "But this is from Prince Norr. I know the King is old and sickly, but I didn't know he had turned decisions like this over to his son."

"Apparently, he has."

Brehira's beautiful eyes squinted at the words. "He says it's not their fight."

"Somehow we'll have to convince them that the Nordoxz won't just stop with us."

"How?"

"I don't know. Read the last one," Brehira said urgently. "That's probably the royal seal of Domari."

Gangus snapped the seal, unfolded the letter and glanced at the words. "No. This is not the Domarians. It's from Queen Antonia of the Nekani and listen to this…she asked if an army of 3,000 be enough?"

"Nekani," Brehira said rolling the name over in her mind. "Oh, the feline humanoids Celio rescued from that Orc camp years ago. But… I never sent the queen a letter."

"I guess Celio must have." Gangus sighed hard. "Well, with Prince Norr's refusal and the Domarian's silence, I suppose we'll have to make do."

"Love, no. We lost two thousand men against the Nordoxz alone. You've got to get the Aenwyns to help us. We need that army. Their archers can pierce the eye of one of those ghastly war dogs' from a hundred yards…probably while drunk on wine."

"So true," Gangus said with a chuckle.

"What about Domari?"

"I'll handle the Domarians," she said.

"Good. I'll call a meeting with my commanders. See if you can locate Olutunji, he's lived in those woods for months. Maybe he can talk some sense into Prince Norr.

"I'll do my best, Love."

Gangus left Brehira in the study while he had a servant summon his high ranking officers.

Brehira got busy sending word to all the trappers and hunters that she needed the presence of Olutunji.

Olutunji had been spending time with the Gunji, a group of Aenwyns who lived deep within the Aenwyn woods. Gunjis were highly spiritual beings, who worshiped and protected nature. The most powerful of them could shapeshift into various animals and had power over animals and plants. They taught those skills to Olutunji.

In the quietness of the woods, Olutunji sat cross-legged meditating when a voice whispered in his ear. His eyes flashed open. "Lady Abram, you say?" The nightingale nodded. "Then take a message to Prince Norr that I desire an audience with him." The bird nodded, tweeted and flew off.

Days later, Brehira walked into Gangus' study where he was pouring over maps of the West. "Abram, Olutunji came through. The Aenwyn prince will be attending the conference."

Gangus smiled. "Ah, that's good news, Love. And give Olutunji my gratitude."

"I will," she said before closing the door behind her.

There were months of planning for the conference. Weeks earlier, Brehira had traveled to Domari with her priestess. With much persuasion from her daughters, Grand Matron Diana, who never traveled outside of Domari, agreed to send Pryah and Alema, top generals of the Domari warrior caste called the "Dedroyles" to represent her.

At Brehira's return, she noticed a slack in the preparations and sternly got behind her servants who quickly began cleaning and polishing. Everything that was wood, metal, or ceramic took on a shine that seemed the envy of the stars. The cooks chose only the best fruit and vegetables, and the finest of eatable beasts were set aside and fatten for the butcher. Everything had to be perfect. In Volari culture, it was considered an insult to allow dignitaries to travel long distances for any reason and not provide them with a reasonable time of stay and the finest of food, drink, and entertainment.

The guest quarters were massive with enough room for each guest's entourage which would include: servants, food and beverage tasters, Medicus and armed guards. Each guest would have their wing of the building with adjoining rooms for servants and guards. Brehira had overseen every detail of the preparations and at the end of it rewarded her servants for their well-doing.

Conference

On the last day of the meeting, after food, exotic teas, and entertainment had noticeably satisfied each guest, the guest attended the conference in the great hall, called Yellow Stone, named for the stones used to build it. The large stones were carried down from the mountain of the same name—packed onto large beast-drawn carts and brought to the settlement.

Inside, beautiful silver wood torch holders lined the walls. The flickering light from the torches meshed with the yellow of the walls which made the room warm and inviting. A large ring of silver torch holders with small lit torches hung low from the ceiling. Around the squared room, large, colorful pillows lined the base boards of the floor and busts of Volarian four fathers sat upon tall, marble stands in each corner. In the middle of the room, was a round, colorful rug. Upon the rug, a round, beige, shiny wood table surrounded by pillowed high back chairs. On the table were several large bowls of every kind of fruit and a silver goblet occupied each place setting.

The round table was suggested so that no man thought himself higher than another by sitting at the head of it. With the guest seated, the servants served wine to settle the mood. Seated were the guests, Gangus, Brehira, General Dinary, his sons Rahshi and Glinas who served under Celio. Seated also were all of Gangus' commanders, including, Celio, Olutunji, Nazi, Kofius, and Lygone.

After a few sips of wine, none of course for Priest Hayman, one of the guest stood, lifted his goblet to Lady Abram and toasted her for her excellent treatment of them as well as the food and entertainment. All raised a goblet in Brehira's direction then drank. Brehira nodded and thanked them. Then she stood and toasted them for being more than gracious guests. After the formalities, Gangus began his speech.

"Priest Hayman, King Pyruss, Queen Antonia, Prince Norr, General Pryah, General Alema, Lady Abram and Commanders of the Guards. It is no secret that many months ago, my army suffered a devastating defeat at the hands of the Nordoxz. I know many of you believe that the Nordoxz is simply my problem and that it has nothing to do with you. There is not much known about these creatures except, they have been moving east rapidly—killing and pillaging regions in their path. Every place their spotted feet trod, they take and dominate. They've defeated and taken over the land and lives of many races, including the Orcs and the Minotaurs, which we defeated in a two-year battle. We lost many men, but the greatest was against the Nordoxz—two thousand men and five hundred horses. The horses were slaughter by beasts we had never even imagined. They called them Bohaus—horrible looking creatures spawned from the depths of Hades."

As Gangus spoke, the servants quietly tipped about filling goblets with wine then tipping away. When a servant tipped about to serve a tasty sweet treat, Brehira got her attention and waved her away. All of the servants hurried off and disappeared.

"I am convinced," Gangus continued, "that these creatures intend to move in on my region; and they are not going to just stop with me, but your kingdom, and your kingdom, and yours, and yours," he said nodding towards each, "will be in grave danger. Priest Hayman, King Pyruss, Generals Pryah and Alema of Domari have agreed to join us; and Queen Antonia, whom I had not the pleasure of meeting before this conference, has graciously offered to send as many as three thousands of her best soldiers to aid us in the war against the Nordoxz." Gangus turned to the queen. "I can't thank you enough, Your Majesty."

The Queen with her chin held high nodded at Gangus for acknowledging her generosity.

"I hope you haven't forgotten," Prince Norr blurted, "I'm only here to lend my expertise in battle strategies. And unless the Qu'Venars, with their awesome magic, joins you, I'm not likely to."

"Aenwyns! It's just like you to accept another man's hospitality then spit in his face."

"What do you mean by that?" Prince Norr asked. "And what do women know of war?"

"What do women know of....I'll have you to know," said an indignant Alema, "I can cut any one of your toy soldiers to pieces before their sword leaves their sheaths."

"Did…did she just call my gallant soldiers who brought down the great city of Demorah…conquered kingdoms and slewed giants… TOYS?"

"Hahaha," bellowed King Pyruss, "I believe she did."

"And what are you laughing at?" Prince Norr snapped. "You bloated pompous."

"Who are you calling a pompous? You have the ears of a rabbit and a brain to match."

The room was now emerged in loud insults foaming from the mouths of the two disputing royals with the Domari generals spurring them on.

"Your Majesties, Generals, Please!" Gangus said rising from his chair. "It's the Nordoxz I need you to fight, not each other."

"Well, she started it," Prince Norr snapped.

Suddenly, King Pyruss got a sudden attack of a cough.

"Are you not well? King Pyruss?" Dinary asked.

King Pyruss spoke in a graveled voice. "It…it must be the dust. It dries my throat so."

Brehira clapped her hands in two quick secessions. One of her servants bounced in the doorway. "More wine for our guest," she ordered. The servant bowed and left quickly. The queen who wasn't used to wine was smiling and found the whole exchange quite amusing.

The servants kept filling the goblets with wine while serving Priest Hayman spiced tea. After seeing how rowdy everyone was behaving, Hayman bid everyone goodnight and was escorted to his chambers. Brehira, seeing that the queen and the generals were a bit overcome, kissed Gangus good night and escorted the women to *their* chambers. After a few more rounds of wine, Nazi rested his head on the table and fell asleep while King Pyruss and Prince Norr forgot their differences and went staggering off arm and arm singing and swilling more wine.

"Good goddess," Dinary said. "How do we know the king and prince won't wake up next to each other cold sober and start cutting each other to pieces?"

"Well…for one," Gangus said, "I have their swords…"

"And two?"

"They'll be too embarrassed."

Gangus and Dinary chuckled loudly. Then the king and prince were separated—Dinary took Prince Norr, and Gangus took King Pyruss and marched them off to their separate chambers.

The next morning, only Priest Haymen joined Gangus and Brehira for breakfast. The other guest slept until midday. King Pyruss and Prince Norr didn't remember a thing about last night, and no one dared to tell them they were hugging and singing. Glancing over at them during dinner made it hard for Brehira and Gangus to keep a straight face.

After dining, the guest returned to Yellow Stone. Gangus had hoped last night's friendliness was not just the result of the wine. But he was wrong. Nothing had changed. The Aenwyns still refused to join unless the Qu'Venars did.

Gangus shook his head in disgust. Well, you've been friends with them long enough...tell me how to get through to them."

"I don't know," the prince said. "They're pretty stubborn. You're going to have to give them something. And knowing them, it's going to have to be a lot."

"I'll go, Father. I believe I can convince the king of the Qu'Venars.

Prince Norr looked upon Dinary with great admiration. "I've heard of your bravery and great battle skills," young Dinary, "but not even you can stand against even the weakest of their spell casters, or survive their mystical forest and make it to the Qu'Venar city. I have learned much about the Qu'Venars during my time with them," Prince Norr continued. "There are things in their region that a sword cannot defeat. That forest reeks of a powerful enchantment; any uninvited guest will be lost, rendered mad or worst. But if you insist," the prince said with a great sigh, "I've been invited to meet King Issicah, perhaps you can accompany me. Seeing me always puts King Issicah in a good mood. You'll need him to be so if there's any hope he'll change his mind."

Gangus thanked Prince Norr then turned to Dinary. "Son, take as many men as you'd like."

"Yes, Father. I will make the necessary arrangements." Dinary hurried from the room.

Chapter Eighteen

Eye of the Dragon

Prince Norr, accompanied by his entourage, led Dinary and twenty of his men including Celio, Olutunji, and the Damari generals and over Dinary's objections, his wife, Princess Lerayah. The two had a heated exchange until Brehira told Dinary she had been secretly training Lerayah in divine gifts. Although Dinary relented, a part of him still objected to the idea of exposing his love to the awaited dangers.

It took twenty-one days on horseback to travel from the settlement to the Qu'Venar kingdom. The travel band gasped when they saw the branches on near-by trees point and grass part to reveal the path to the city.

Although most of the enigmatic and adept Qu'Venar resided in Nekanian lands, most believe they originated somewhere within the Entrydal Forest, next to the Aenwyn people. The forest's reputation truly preceded itself: sitting just east of the Haunted Wasteland, and as colorful and gorgeous as the Qu'Venar's claims of being aloof and scientific. The area attracted many nature-lovers for its idyllic community and serene Emerald Lake where the forest Qu'Venar lived simply, in small homes nestled in between the trees, though most were powerful mages, residing and studying in the arcane tower of Sharian. The spire lay on the lake's edge; its beauty was said to be so enticing that — to the irritation of Sharian's sorcerers — travelers were often tempted to stay until next sunrise.

As the band traveled through the forest, Dinary, who was leading the band, stepped on a crimsoned patch of ground that resembled red clay. He bent to touch the strange dirt when arrows whizzed above his head, missing him by inches. "What the...?" Dinary blurted.

"Young Dinary!" Prince Norr yelled. "For god's sake man, don't stand up...crawl backward on your knees."

Dinary did as told. "What the Hades was that?" he said standing.

"Son, you're moving too fast. You can't just walk where you please. Some parts of this forest are what the Qu'Venars consider sacred ground, and we must get permission from the regional wizard to move beyond a certain point.

"And you know such wizards?" Olutunji asked.

"That I do…and is why I'm traveling with you. You must walk where I tell you."

"Apologies, Good Prince," Dinary said. "I didn't mean to get ahead of you. I'm just anxious to get to the city."

"I quite understand, son. But let us do so in one piece," the prince said smiling.

Dinary nodded with a smile and followed the prince to a gloomy patch of ground that spread bright as soon as Norr's foot touched the darkness. Well up ahead, a wizard appeared stony-faced dressed in colorful attire of blue-green, orange and bright yellow. He smacked his six-foot staff against the ground and asked of what authority brought them there. Prince Norr stepped forward and spoke words only the wizard understood, and the colorfully clad man stepped aside. This incident was repeated several times. Because of the prince's knowledge of the forest, there were no encounters with the creatures during the journey. However, Dinary knew coming there on his own wouldn't be that easy next time. The band continued to travel until they reached a little village with common houses, shops, and small buildings.

"Why are we stopping here?" Princess Lerayah asked.

"We've been traveling for hours," Olutunji said irritated. "Where is this city?"

"Calm yourselves," Prince Norr urged them, "We can't see her, but she sees us."

"Who?" Dinary asked.

"The sorcerer. She's looking us over before letting us in."

"In? In where?" Lerayah asked, squinting at the simple little village.

Suddenly a glow grew over the little village and when the glitter subsided, there before them stood the most beautiful city they had ever seen. It was the city of Entrydal sitting by the sparkling waters of Emerald Lake. Eighty-six thousand Qu'Venars live there over five acres. The city bustled with excitement and its beauty was overwhelming. Dinary and the band were immediately taken to meet the Council of Ten Magi, but to their disappointment, King Issicah did not attend. The King, however, kept his meeting with Prince Norr and could see that the Prince who feared for his people's safety, really wanted to join Gangus in the battle against the Nordoxz. The King felt bad standing in his way. So he thought up a game he would play for his amusement. It would

144

be a game he knew his opponent could not win. That way, he could refuse Gangus, but still stay in good graces with the Aenwyns.

To Prince Norr's surprise, King Issicah ordered that Dinary and a small group be brought before him. Dinary, Olutunji, Celio and the Domari generals bowed before the king.

"You sent for us Your Majesty?" Dinary asked straightening.

"Yes. I've thought the matter over. There is only one way I will join you," Issicah began.

"Really?" Dinary asked with relief.

"As everyone of importance knows, my kingdom is used to winning. I've never lost a battle. Your army was beaten badly by the Nordoxz. I think you lost because your army was weak. Just one of my Magi could have destroyed them. I don't think your soldiers are worthy of my help."

Dinary squinted at the king but was careful with his tongue. "With all due respect, Your Majesty, that's not only wrong, but it's also insulting."

"I didn't mean to insult you, General. I'm just looking out for my kingdom's reputation. We can't afford to lower our standards with such weak alliances."

"I don't know what you want from me."

"A quest."

"What kind of quest?" Dinary asked.

"For generations, there has been talk of a precious emerald stone, the size of my fist, called The Eye of the Dragon. It was stolen from an ancient tribe called the Mycide that was wiped out by an unknown force centuries ago. It was said to have been carried off into the Haunted Wastelands. But the ones who carried it there were never heard from again. It has been said that the Eye is guarded day and night by ghastly creatures. Select your bravest men or women," he said nodding at the generals, "to lead a small army to fetch it. Bring me this stone, and I'll send three of my best Magi for your father's cause…and not a Magus more," the king ended with a smirk.

"As my father told you," Dinary said. "This isn't just our cause. Haven't you been listening?" Dinary reminded the king that the Nordoxz would take his land also if not stopped. Plus, he told the king that he thought the quest was the most ridiculous thing he'd ever heard. But King Issicah said it was his price.

The Princess, fearing it was a trick that would endanger her husband and the band, protested loudly. "I don't like this quest," she snapped. "And what of this…this Haunted Wasteland?"

"It is called that," Prince Norr explained, "because the people's hearts were so stained with evil, that when the gods destroyed them for their wickedness, they defied death and became the undead; now the gods have no power over them."

"And this is where you want to send my husband? You're not even sure if the stone is truth or myth."

But Dinary had heard from other races that such a stone existed though he doubted the king's story of its origin. Dinary, anxious to have the Qu'Venar's help blurted, "All right, I'll go." The princess said she wouldn't hear of it. But Dinary stood his ground and stated that the rest of his band didn't have to take the suicide mission.

Celio told Dinary that he wasn't going to let him go without him. Olutunji volunteered. The generals looked at each other and hunched their shoulders. "Who knows, it might be fun," Pryah joked. "Count us in."

"So, then it's settled," King Issicah said with a sinister grin.

Later that day, King Issicah summoned Dinary again and handed him a map marking the way to the Haunted Wasteland. It was a map to sudden death; for rarely if ever did anyone returned from that ghastly world.

The King allowed Dinary and the band to stock up with enough supplies for the journey to the Wasteland territory. It took the band ten days traveling on horseback, but when the horses became spooked with only a half mile to go inside the desert, the men had to make a fifteen-day journey to Modos ruin haunted city on foot. Dinary, Princess Lerayah, and ten soldiers joined them in the desert. Celio, Olutunji, the Domari generals and the others stayed behind to care for the horses.

After traveling several miles inside the desert, Dinary noticed a slight wind blowing. Within minutes, the wind picked up, and after several more, a full sand storm had engulfed them. They placed thick cloths over their mouths and noses, but a thinner one over their eyes so they could still see. The storm blew at their backs like rough hands were pushing them—perhaps, hurrying them towards their uncertain fate.

The small band entwined their arms tightly and pushed against the wind. In spite of the cloth coverings, sand got into their eyes, ears, nose, and mouth. The sand began to weigh them down and get into their water supply and food.

Much had to be thrown away; and some, the storm carried away. Finally, unable to fight against the wind, they decided to gather themselves into a tight ball on the ground—putting what little food and water they managed to hang on to in the middle of the circle and wait out the storm. After what seemed an hour, the storm ceased. Shaking the sand from their garments and packings, they journeyed on. A few hours before night, they stopped and set up camp. As they sat before the fire eating dried figs and swilling tea, Rhico, one of the soldiers yelled and threw a fig at something he thought he saw. The fig slowly sank into the sand and was gone. Rhico grabbed his sword and scrambled to his feet.

Princess Lerayah laughed. "There's nothing there you big baby."

"Stop laughing; I thought I saw something."

"Probably your shadow," the Princess said with a chuckle.

"And you fed the sand our last fig," said one of the soldiers.

"Maybe you should throw it some tea to wash it down," said another soldier. Everyone laughed.

"That's enough, you jug-heads," Dinary said to the men while trying not to laugh. "It's all right, Rhico. We all are a little spooked."

The men grumbled in agreement; however, the princess' shoulders shook from trying to contain her laugh.

"Anyway," Dinary said yawning, "we better get some sleep."

The men grabbed their bedding and settled down for the night. Princess Lerayah snuggled up to Dinary and rested her head on his chest. He pulled the covers over her shoulders and held her tightly as they slept.

*****

Pieces of darkness crept across the barren landscape. The abandon desert sat so still beneath the full moon sky. The silence was deafening—as if the bodies of the once living were screaming without breath from the depths of the sands. The princess wavered between sleep and awake as odd shapes slithered to and fro. Am I dreaming? She thought. Then an evil stench pierced her senses; she slowly raised her eye lids and gasped when her eyes fell upon a dozen undead that had snatched one of their soldiers away from the rest of the band and had partially eaten him down to the bone. In shock, he had not screamed; and when he tried, the creatures silenced his heart.

Lerayah jolted Dinary awake when she tore herself away from his arms and shot to her feet. He frowned then followed her gaze right to the undead.

Warren W. Randall, Jr.

Dinary reached for his sword and jumped up from his bedding. He yelled to his men who through sleep-filled eyes, staggered to their feet. Each grabbed their weapons, and all stood ready—for what, Dinary wasn't sure since the creatures had no flesh. More skeletons floated out of the sand—followed by a multitude that stood facing the band with a sword in each bony hand.

One of the captains shouted to Dinary. "General, what do we do? They're already dead."

Dinary had seen something like these ghastly things before—years ago on the ghost ship. He had come too late to join his comrades in the fight with the skeletons, but just in time to battle the demonic wooden statue and gallantly defeated it while the crew stood in awe. Before Dinary could answer him, Princess Lerayah yelled to them that she had blessed their swords as they slept and for them not to be afraid.

As the dead and the living squared off, dark slime dripped from the bones of the creatures and the blood-red balls of their eyes blazed upon the soldiers who stood ready to die for each other. Dinary shot forward with a battle cry, his neckless glowing—followed by Rhico and his men. Fearlessly, they ran straight into the multitude—swords clinking and sparkling under the moonlight. The blessed swords took off the skeletal heads and immediately the fleshless bodies turned to dust. Dinary's sword did not turn them to dust, but he could wipe out three at a time. The princess, however, with her divine powers in full capacity stood back from the battle and took out dozens of skeletons at a time until there was nothing but piles of ashes upon the sands and the rest of the undead shot back beneath the surface from whence they came.

The band stayed awake the rest of the night. Princess Lerayah healed the men's wounds and placed a shroud of protection around herself and them, but the undead didn't return that night.

With one man down and ten days to go before reaching Modos ruin city, the band set out early in the morning. Two days into the journey and another sand storm bedeviled them for hours. More food and tea was ruin or carried off with the wind. The princess' powers provided plenty of water, but the dried goods were scares. They began to ration the bread.

"Bet you could use that fig right about now…huh Rhico," the princess said grinning.

"Ha ha," Rhico scoffed. "Eat my sand," he said walking ahead of her.

Dinary shook his head at Lerayah's naughtiness.

148

The Chronicles of Bethica

Six more days to go and the band was getting too weak to travel just on small portions of bread. Then one of the men shouted something from up ahead. He'd found a sack and came running back with teeth flashing.

"Look what I found," he said opening the large sack. The sack belonged to them. The wind had blown the sack with figs, dates, and bread miles ahead of them. And so tightly packed, there was no trace of sand. With bellies half full, the men took a nap and the princess, who wasn't hungry, decided she'd keep watch. The men napped longer than usual, and the princess turned to wake them with a tease when she noticed foam dripping in the corners of their mouths, and they didn't appear to be breathing.

Naturally, she went to her husband first and slapped him several times to wake him. When he didn't respond, Lerayah said to herself, "Great goddess, poison." She quickly held her hands over Dinary's abdomen. With his eyes still closed, he jolted to a sitting position and vomited until he was red in the face. She did the same for each man, and they were all healed. She created plenty of water for them to drink to flush any remaining toxins from their bodies.

"What happened?" Dinary asked, his voice gravelly.

"Nothing is what it seems in this god-forsaken place," She said. "That wind isn't a wind at all, but an entity with an evil mind. Something put us under a mirage." The princess took a blade and sliced opened the sack they had eaten from, and there were thick green maggots. And when they looked at what they had vomited, on the ground were also maggots.

"I'm going to be sick again," one of the men said making a face at the maggots. He ran off to vomit again. But it was only fresh water.

"We've got to get that Emerald and get the Hades out of here before we starve to death," Rhico said angrily.

"We have enough rationings," Dinary said. "And with our divine gifts, we won't have to spend a lot of our energy fighting whatever awaits us."

"Thank the gods the princess is with us," Rhico said.

The men grumbled in agreement, and Dinary looked upon his wife with pride.

After the men had felt better, they journeyed on to Modos with only twelve hours to go. Another sand storm, but this time they held on to their rations. Dinary decided to camp, but Lerayah told him they shouldn't chance it because she had used up her powers for that day and they should keep moving before it got dark and the undead attacked them again.

149

"I may have enough for a ghoul or two," the princess said, but not for multiple demons."

Each took a few pinches of bread and drank water then headed towards Modos. Just a few miles outside the city, one of the men hung back to relieve himself. The band, unaware he had stopped, kept moving until they heard a yell. All snatched their heads towards the scream and saw a Wraith sucking the soul of the soldier. Lerayah held out her hand, but there was nothing. The band ran back to him as fast as they could. The Wraith, dressed in a worn, dirty white wedding gown with a ragged hemline that looked as if dragged through the mud, smelled of rotting flesh. It had no feet or legs, and it floated horizontally. It had a torn, thin veil over its fossil face, with stringy white hair nearly as long as the veil and yellow eyes that glowed like lamps in the dark. The men fought it away from the soldier, but it was too late. The Wraith shot up into mid-air and disappeared, leaving behind a dried up spread of wrinkled skin where a man used to be.

"No wonder they call this place the Haunted Wasteland," Rhico said. "I hate it."

The Wasteland was a barren, desolate, truly forsaken area. This once rich and thriving region, occupying the northwestern corner of the Northern Mountains, and home to the twin cities Harromog and Modos, was considered by many to be the pinnacles of Bethican culture. But the citizens of Harromog and Modos grew prideful. They openly rebuked the gods and basked in their sins, and legend proclaimed that the gods sent upon them a rain of divine fire that not only reduced the cities to piles of rubble but salted the very earth around them.

Nothing grew in the Haunted Wasteland. It was the only part of Bethica that could truly be called barren and lifeless. Rolling fog coiled around the feet of the shambling, moaning city; the undead was doomed to wander forever under a suffocating cloud-covered sky. Every herb, every seed, and plant placed in the soil were choked and spit out of the ground. For the people of Harromog and Modos, the Haunted Wasteland became the result of the ultimate price they paid to the gods. And for the Abramatic Kingdom and the rest of Bethica, this region was made to stand as a grim reminder to never think oneself above divinity.

Nightfall came and went quickly. It was two men down, another day and the princess had her full divine powers. She blessed the weapons and put a hedge of protection around herself and the band again. But as soon as they entered the city of Modos, they were viciously attacked by zombies. A sword through the head or the whacking off of the head destroyed them. The princess only needed to raise her hand, and multiple zombies exploded into tiny pieces.

Grateful for no casualties among them, they headed to an under cavern that led to the tomb of The Eye of the Dragon. They entered the mouth of the cave and watched their shadows dissolve into the darkness. The cave walls were jagged from the floor to the ceiling and stretched fifty feet upward. Their feet hit sand stones that littered the floor. Decaying air filled their lungs. Lerayah stopped ever so often and concentrated heavily on sensing evil. Having sense none, she and the band moved on.

As they journeyed further, one of the soldiers stepped on—what looked like, a dead tree branch, but when he tried to step off, the branch curled like a snake, wrapped around his ankle and rose with him into the air, dangling him by his ankle fifty feet off the stone floor.

"Get me down!" he yelled.

"Hold on," the princess yelled up to him. She would use her powers against the demonic plant, and the men would stand under him to catch him when he fell. The princess raised her hand but suddenly, right out of thin air, the Wraith shot towards him to suck his soul.

"Help me! No! No! Go away you flea-bitten old hag!"

The Wraith kept bobbing in and out, trying to get to his face to suck out his soul. But this time the princess shot out her hand and the Wraith burst into a rain of black ashes. Then the princess turned her power against the plant that had wrapped itself around the soldier's body and was squeezing the life out of him. Energy shot from her hand, and it burst into a black puff of smoke and disappeared.

"Aah," the soldier screamed as he fell fifty feet. But the men caught him over their heads.

With the soldier safely on the ground, they all chuckled and blew out breaths of relief when suddenly the floor opened under them, and they went crashing to a deeper level of the cave. They all landed on a pile of human skulls. Dinary fell back against the wall, and it moved several inches inward which released a thick, black wall that came thundering down, and separated him from the group.

"Dinary!," the princess yelled. But he couldn't hear her through the thick wall.

"Hey! Get me out." But they couldn't hear him. Then the floor slowly began to part, and Dinary saw that soon there would be no floor at all. Through the small opening, he could see a pitch black endless drop. "Hey, I need to get out of here. Can anybody hear me?" He yelled banging on the wall. The floor opened wider and had his back against the wall with his toes hanging off the edge of the opened floor. "Hey! Out there? Lerayah, Rhico." Dinary looked up and all around him then called on the gods.

"Dinary, hold on, we'll get you out," The princess said. They began to feel along the wall in hopes of finding a way to bring the wall back up and free him. Panic-stricken, Dinary screamed for them to hurry. The band kept feeling around various areas of the wall with no success. Only Dinary's heels were on the floor with more than half of the bottom of his foot facing the black hole. "Hang in there," Rhico yelled. Seconds ticked by, Lerayah and the men continued to feel along the wall. "We're trying, honey, Stay calm," she said. But behind the wall there was silence. Seconds more, and the group effort appeared useless. Finally, the princess pushed on a portion of the wall and heard the click under her fingers. "I found it?" She shouted. The wall slid up with a roar. But Dinary had vanished along with the floor. The princess and the others stepped forward and gazed down into the black Abyss. She felt her heart when it skipped, and the men gasped. Disbelief marked their faces.

"Well, you gonna stand there, or get me down from here?"

The princess and the men looked up, and Dinary was barely holding on to a short ledge near the ceiling of the confined space. Lerayah stepped back, and Rhico reached up and grabbed his ankle. The other men grabbed parts of his clothing, and together they pulled him in.

Exhausted from hanging on Dinary sat on the floor to catch his breath, "I was screaming. What took you so long?"

"We were screaming too," Rhico said.

"A thank you would be nice," Lerayah said.

"Thank you," he said. "Now let's go find that darn stone and get the hades out of here." Dinary got up off the floor.

"Well, I think we go this way," Rhico said, heading right.

"No, let's go this way," Dinary said.

"I think you're wrong," the princess said.

"No, it's this way," Dinary said. He stumbled against the wall, and it moved in a few inches. "Oh no not again," Dinary cried out. But this time the wall slowly roared up, and there sat the head of a dragon and in the middle of its forehead sat the magnificent Emerald stone. The princess and the men stood with their mouths open, gazing at the royal beauty while Dinary took out his dagger and carefully plucked out the stone. He turned holding it in one hand like he was cradling a premature baby. They all finally found their voices and began laughing and hugging each other. Each took turns holding and admiring the stone. They celebrated some more then returned the stone to Dinary who carefully placed it in a silk cloth he had brought to wrap it in; that is, if he'd found it. Expressing their happiness, they giggled and started the short journey out of the cave, when the sound of rocks crumbling made them look over their shoulders. Removing the stone had made the dragon come alive, and it was trying to wrestle its body from the wall to reclaim it.

"Run!" the princess yelled. This was not an undead, and Princess Lerayah couldn't destroy or hold it at bay. The Qu'Venar Magi had claimed that a spell kept most things not human from leaving the cave. Why the Magi failed to disclose what would happen when the stone was removed was something the band would surely take up with them once they got back. If they could get out before it freed itself, they would be safe. But the cave was also crumbling and huge chunks, like boulders that fell from the cave ceiling had blocked their way. Dinary and Lerayah's quick exit from the cave was slowed as they tried to find a way around the falling rocks. They caught up with the soldiers, and all ran off together towards the exit that was around the corner and up ahead. Just before rounding the corner, Dinary had looked back over his shoulder and saw that the dragon's long tail was still a part of the cave wall. Then one yank, and it was free. Its massive body was the size of a battle ship—its tail as long as a mule train. It roared towards them spitting fire, but several large chunks of the cave ceiling crashed down upon its head and back—slowing its advance. The band could see the exit far up ahead and could taste their freedom as their feet ate up the distance, but a chunk of ceiling fell right in front of the exit blocking their way.

"Holy stars! There's got to be another way out." the princess yelled.

"This way, I think," Rhico said, running ahead. They rounded a corner and saw a stream of sun shining on the stone floor. They tore ahead then stopped suddenly when the giant shadow of the dragon fell between them and their freedom. The band turned and ran in the opposite direction with an injured dragon limping along behind them. If they could stay clear of its fire, they would make it out safely.

"Rhico," Dinary yelled, "are you sure you know where you're going?"

"I can smell the undead in the sand; we're going the right way," the princess yelled.

As they rushed to the mouth of the cave, the dragon blew fire that singed their hair and clothes. They turned the corner running as fast as they could. The roar of the dragon was getting closer. The princess could feel the smelly air on her face. The dragon turned the corner and was coming up on them fast. It blew its fiery breath, and the princess' garment went up in a blaze. Dinary tore the garment off of her, and they continued on.

They shot down the long stretch of the cave towards the opening— the dragon right on their heels, as they bolted through the huge opening; the dragon shot another blaze that set a soldier on fire; he tumbled down to the ground. Rhico turned back to rescue him, but the fallen soldier yelled to him, "Save yourself!" as he tried to beat out the flames. Rhico wouldn't listen and started back then Dinary grabbed him. "Rhico, you can't save him, brother." Reluctantly, Rhico turned and ran with Dinary out of the mouth of the cave. They looked back and saw their brave comrade, smoke coming from his clothes, fighting for his life—gallantly cutting and stabbing the dragon with all of his might until it took him into its mouth and bit him in half.

The band ran as fast as they could to a safe distance far from the cave. They all fell on the sands panting and trying to catch their breaths. The princess laid her head against Dinary's chest and cried for their brave comrade. Several soldiers covered her half nakedness with their garments.

Back to the horses, Celio, Olutunji, the Domari generals and the rest of the band welcomed them with cheers when seeing they were alive and in possession of the great emerald.

In The City of Entrydal, they were given a heroes' welcome, and the story of their brave adventure spread throughout the Qu'Venar Kingdom. But King Issicah was a heartless king. Not expecting Dinary to succeed, the king was caught off guard. He took the emerald and days later, sent Dinary, Lerayah and the soldiers to the east wing of the castle to a big banquet in their honor, they were told. But when they entered the room, everything began to glitter, and when the glitter cleared, they found themselves outside the Qu'Venar Forest. Dinary couldn't believe it. The princess was right all along. The soldiers were steaming mad. Everything they'd been through: the sand storms; the hunger; the danger; the fighting; the loss of good men, had all been—for nothing.

Chapter Nineteen

War of the Gods

Barthod, Shaman to the Nordoxz Emperor Vaganor, sat with his legs crossed under him chanting in front of a magical fire. Suddenly, Barthod fell dead as he often did before Nelchael, the god of death, appeared before him. The living is bombarded with emotions, sights, sounds, and smells that distract them from seeing the truer reality than what the mortal senses can detect.

The Shaman's spirit rose before a throne of fire then quickly bowed before Nelchael who sat upon the flames. Nelchael appeared as a preserved corpse. His greyish-blue skin covered a skeletal frame with every bone in his face outlined under the skin. The balls of his eyes were black as coals and were sunk deep within his eye sockets. Clothed in a black silk robe, with his face buried deep within its hood, he majestically sat as the fire crackled around him and black smoke hovered above him like a cloud.

Barthod trembled as he spoke. "Oh great god of death I come before you with an urgency. The humanoid, Gangus has managed to talk many of Bethica's races into forging a powerful army. He has faced us alone, and we barely beat him. Now, we must face an even mightier army of many races.

Nelchael's voice was as a mighty wind storm. "WHAT IS YOUR RE-QUEST, SHAMAN?!"

"That you send an assassin spirit to kill Gangus, My Lord."

The black balls of Nelchael's eyes burned into Barthod's eyes and scorched his soul. "GO! I WILL CONSIDER YOUR REQUEST!"

"Thank you Lord Nelchael," he said. Then the Shaman's spirit returned to him; he opened his eyes and set up with a sinister smile.

*****

Dinary stormed into his father's study causing Gangus to jump.

"Dinary, you're as bad as your mother. You scared the dickens out of me. Doesn't anybody bother to knock anymore?"

"I'm sorry father, but King Issicah is a snake. You…you can't believe one word he says. He's not a being of honor. He's ah…ah dirty rotten…"

"Hold it, son...slow down."

Dinary took a deep breath then told Gangus about the quest and what the Qu'Venar King had done. Gangus expressed how disappointed he was but said there was good news. The Aenwyns had agreed to fight against the Nordoxz. "Don't know what changed their minds," Gangus said. But he later learned that Prince Norr had become angry when he'd discovered two days into Dinary's journey to the Haunted Wastelands that the quest was a hoax and that King Issicah had no intentions of changing his mind about joining the battle and that it had all been an amusing game. He further learned that they had argued about it and Prince Norr stormed out of the castle and went home.

With weeks of planning ahead of them, Dinary, Princess Lerayah and the soldiers who had accompanied them on the quest, soon dismissed the treachery of the king. As Gangus and the leaders of the races met on occasion to plan their strategy, miles away in the Qu'Venar Forest, King Issicah's wicked ways were about to catch up to him and have his perfect world turned upside-down.

*****

The noonday sky was dark with clouds and the air hot and sticky; thousands of flies swarmed over the battle field where brains, blood, and decapitated bodies lay stinking upon the ground. At the end of the battle field, Gangus and The Thunder Guards which consisted of Volarians, Timbakni, Engamars, Aenwyns, and Nekani, stood wide-legged with their various weapons. Sweat burned their eyes like sea water that dripped down from the open pores of their blood and dirt stained faces. All around them was nothing but stench, the blur of colorful war banners and groans from dying men. The sound of the battle horn barely registered in some bloody ears. While above the heat and sweat and stench rose a cloud of uncertainty among The Thunder Guards who had suffered severe losses.

"At my signal unleash the Bohaus," General Tarus commanded his captain. Tarus was the elder son of Emperor Vaganor, next in line to the Nordoxz throne and much too valuable to die in battle. He stayed well-guarded in the Western Hills and peered over the battle field and was pleased. The war had lasted several days at a time over a period of eleven months. The Nordoxz had cut the Thunder Guards off from Shukuna Lake causing their horses to die of thirst and had also pushed the Guards dangerously close to the Minotaur territory.

Because Gangus had barely cheated death many times, the captains of the Guards insisted that he not lead this time, but Gangus wouldn't hear of it. He rallied his men. "You are not fighting for me," Gangus said, "or the gods, or for mere victory. Remember our loved ones who died crossing the Endless Ocean; remember the Drake, the Island of Gorr, the Ogres, Orcs, the Minotaurs, the thirty-seven years it took to build our city. Are we going just to let these spotted beasts run us off our land?"

"NO!" the men shouted with their weapons raised.

"Then, go! Let us die like Volarians. And send those bloody animals to the fiery pits of Hades!"

"Ahhhhhh!" The Thunder Guards cried out running towards the Nordoxz who were roaring towards the Guards; but out in front of them were the Bohaus, eating up the ground with their six legs, their noses flared, their fangs dripping with saliva. Little did the Nordoxz realize that unlike the battle before against the Volarian archers, that the Bohaus were no match for the Aenwyns who could shoot the horns off a deer and not break its stride.

The Bohaus thundered towards the Guards; the Aenwyns drew back their bows and aimed. The sky immediately turned black with arrows moving nearly at the speed of light. The sound as the arrows left their bows was deafening, like a million flies buzzing overhead. To the Nordoxz's shock, every arrow met its mark—a hundred Bohaus fell instantly dead, an arrow pierced each eye and struck the brain. While the Aenwyns reloaded, the Nekani leaped upon the backs of the Bohaus and dug their feet and hand claws into the beast—sinking their fangs into the back of their necks and breaking it. Dinary's necklace glowed, he cut down several beasts with his sword, but another struck him from behind, landing him face down in the dirt. As Dinary's, necklace continued glowing, he quickly turned over on his back and rammed his sword through the heart of the beast. Up on his feet, Dinary turned and saw Gangus with two Bohaus attacking him, he ran to aid his father, but Celio beat him to it. With his mighty shield, he struck the beast, knocking it to the ground then ran his blade through its brain.

Olutunji had shapeshifted into a Bohaus and had attacked and killed several Nordoxz from behind the lines. When other Bohaus discovered, by smell, that he wasn't one of them, they attacked and ran him off the field. Olutunji, badly injured, staggered off and fell into the arms of Brehira who healed him.

With all of their fighting, it still wasn't enough to drive the Nordoxz back. Then suddenly, a high pitched battle cry and the ground turned brown with the beautiful tan bodies of the notorious Domari army, the Dedroyles. Ten thousand women behind silver shields were swinging spears that the average man had to lift with two hands. Stabbing Bohaus and Nordoxz alike; in hours— with the help of the Dedroyles, the Thunder Guards drove the Nordoxz army into The Western Woods. The Nordoxz found that they were no match for the Engamars who tore into them with their mighty axes and hammers. They sliced into heads, chopped off arms and legs. The Engamars double-platted shields blocked every blow from the Nordoxz's weapons.

Enraged by the turn of the battle, the Emperor commanded Barthod, the Shaman, to summon the Cavemorphs that were seven-feet, dark gray creatures with the head of a buffalo, a wide black mane and twenty-four-inch needle-point antelope horns. They stood on four muscular arms and at the end of its expenditures were split hooves. Their eyes were large, round blue lights; they had flared nostrils and three-inch fangs. They roared like lions, and the ground shook when they moved. The Cavemorphs bolted toward the guards with the speed of horses, and Gangus' eyes flashed wide. "Holy gods of Bethica."

*****

King Issicah sat admiring the Eye of the Dragon as he often did. He had no regrets for how he dishonestly obtained it. The glittering emerald sparkled like a green sun as he rolled it between his thumb and fingers. The blood of the three Volarians soldiers who had died in the Haunted Wasteland cried out to Raziel, the god of their destinies, but he was helpless to avenge them. However, in Bethica, few bad deeds go unpunished, and fate was about to step in.

"King Issicah!" shouted a servant storming into the King's chambers. "We're being invaded, Your Majesty."

"Invaded? That's impossible. No one can come into the forest uninvited. Invaded by whom?"

"Not whom, Your Majesty. What?"

"Speak plainly, you fool."

"Ah…ah…strange six-legged animals. They're trampling down our beautiful plants and have killed several of our citizens."

"But how did they get in?"

"I don't know Your Majesty. Shall I call upon the Maji?"

"No! The Maji's magic would destroy the forest. Summon the Aenwyns. Tell them it's urgent."

"Yes, My Lord."

It eluded the Qu'Venars' knowledge that unlike other creatures, Bohaus bore an extremely high sense of smell and not fooled by the magic of the forest that hid the city; it easily found the Qu'Venars with its scent. Nelchael had sent the Bohaus at the request of the Shaman, Barthod who feared that the Qu'Venar king would change his mind and join the Thunder Guards. But it backfired. The Aenwyns came and struck down the Bohaus with their bows, but refused to stay and guard the city unless the king joined the Guards against the Nordoxz. King Issicah, grateful to Prince Norr's help, was only too happy to change his mind.

When the Qu'Venars pranced onto the battle field, King Issicah couldn't believe his eyes. There were Cavemorphs everywhere. Gangus' staff had caused a sweeping wind to blow against the Nordoxz, keeping many at bay, but he had used up most of the staff's energy, and it was growing weak.

Dinary managed to cut several Cavemorphs to pieces but was still overwhelmed by many more. The Domari Dedroyles had speared many Nordoxz and Cavemorphs though they lost 800 women in the hard fought battle. While Brehira's priestess' were healing and resurrecting, mostly the Dedroyles, Celio was healing and blessing his men. Though many Cavemorphs lay in pools of blood with Aenwyn arrows through their eyes, the battle field was still dominated by the enormous creatures. Then Gangus' staff gave out, and the Nordoxz advanced with a vengeance; it was total pandemonium. Hundreds of Nekanis had been ripped apart and impaled on the sharp antelopes of the Cavemorphs.

King Issicah ordered three of his Maji to take to the air; they hovered over the battle field with their hands raised. From the palm of one shot fire, while the other two threw lightning. The lightning struck hundreds of Cavemorphs and lit up their bodies, revealing their inside skeletal frames. The fire Maji had hundreds of Nordoxz hopping and rolling on the ground to put out the flames. Many died screaming and on fire.

The battle raged on for nearly two years with heavy losses on both sides. The Emperor grew impatient with the outcomes of each battle. One night Nelchael was summoned to make good on his promise.

Brehira's body shifted beneath the covers. She heard a small voice that woke her. It was not a human voice. She looked around, and Gangus was not beside her. She had left him earlier in the Command Tent sitting and looking over some battle plans. She had kissed him and gone to bed alone. Wrapping a cloak around her shoulders, Brehira ventured out into the night air. When she reached the tent, she gasped loudly. The guards that had surrounded the Command Tent were all mummified—their bodies white and shriveled liked dried figs.

"Gangus!" Brehira screamed. She rushed into the tent and found Gangus on his back paralyzed, and staring wildly into the dead eyes of a Wraith that was sucking his soul. Brehira immediately bound the Wraith in an invisible binding, but the creature was just as strong as Brehira. She broke free, attacked Brehira who suffered scratches and bite marks on her face and neck. Brehira raised her hand and drove the creature hard across the ground. The Wraith recovered and sailed towards Brehira in midair, crashing into her and knocking her down. Brehira scrambled to her feet and prayed a stronger binding, but nothing Brehira did seemed to work against the Wraith. Finally, Brehira commanded all things around her to obey. Suddenly, a portal, red with spitting fire, opened in the air. Wider and wider it opened, and a blazing tongue shot out from the pit, wrapped itself around the Wraith and pulled it into its flaming mouth. As the Wraith growled and struggled, the portal closed and disappeared. Brehira stumbled back and took a deep breath then ran to Gangus and healed him.

Emperor Vaganor stood seething when he learned that Gangus was not dead. He screamed at his Shamans. "What do I have you around for? You're supposed to be able to call on the powers of darkness. Yet this…this, bloody vermin is still alive!"

The Shamans stood trembling before the Emperor. Vaganor squinted at them. His black eyes chilled their bones. "I have a good mind to feed you to my eight-legged pets," he said, his mouth twisted in a hideous grin.

Sweat poured from the Shamans as their knees weakened. "Please My Lord. It…it was his wife," Barthod, the leader said. "We…we did not anticipate her interference, My Lord."

"What about his wife?" the Emperor barked.

"She is very powerful, My Lord. But, never worry, we will summon the very darkness itself to serve us. Not even she will be able to survive."

"SEE TO IT, THEN!"

"Yes, Great Lord," Barthod said. The Shamans continuously bowed as they backed out of the Emperor's presence.

Emperor Vaganor had under estimated the Thunder Guards. Now he would send his Red Hordes, the deadliest of his Nordoxz. Many said that they were the offspring of innocent maidens and Fallen Angels who had taken advantage of them. Each had stood against a Cavemorph with nothing but a two-edged sword and cut the creatures to pieces. They feared nothing and no one and had never lost a battle. They were the ones who captured and trained the Bohaus and were the only ones the Bohaus were afraid to attack. There were songs written about the Red Hordes—about how the trees uprooted and scattered, and how the grass hid beneath the earth when the Hordes marched passed them. And as if they weren't evil enough, the Red Hordes had their own Shamans who were ordained by the evil god Nelchael.

This last battle would not be fought with swords, spears, axes, hammers or bows, but with fire, wind, lightning, rain and divine gifts. Ordinary creatures and humanoids would not fight the battle, but those who were masters of the elements and had direct links to the gods.

Gangus stood with his staff facing the Red Hordes and their Shamans. Brehira stood at Gangus' side. The Qu'Venar Maji stood at Gangus and Olutunji. Celio and his men with their newly blessed swords stood beside Princess Lerayah who stood next to Dinary, his necklace glowing like a bright star. Emperor Vaganor sat high on his horse; upon his head rested a gold plated skull crown with ruby stones in its eye sockets. He smiled (at what he believed) was the last of Gangus and his pathetic army.

Barthod led the Shamans in summoning the elements to fight against the Guards. A mighty wind swooped down upon the field where several of Celio's soldiers were lifted up into a whirlwind. Gangus pointed his staff, and his wind pierced the whirlwind, and the soldiers dropped to the ground in a daze. Gangus' wind was so powerful that the Emperor's horse rocked backward.

"Do something, you idiots!" Vanagor shouted.

A Shaman commanded the trees to attack. Towering Bowthorpe Oak uprooted and thunder towards the Guards. The Dedroyles threw spears, but no effect. The Aenwyns shot their arrows that whizzed through the branches, striking leaves but little else. Several trees shot out their roots that wrapped around the neck of soldiers and snapped off their head. Other trees deliberately fell upon the soldiers and crushed them—ten, twenty at a time. The Maji shot fire from their hands that was so hot, it consumed the giant Bowthorpes and reduced them to ashes in seconds. The Maji threw huge fire balls at the Nordoxz army that spooked their horses and made them rear up causing their riders to tumble to the ground. But the Emperor's horse was steadied by protectors of the Emperor and Vanagor remained seated. The Shaman summoned clouds out of nowhere that burst with a deafening clap of thunders, and the rain poured like buckets from the sky. The rain quickly turned into a flood and with a current that threatened to wash Gangus' army away, but Gangus sent a wind that parted the water so that his army stood on wet grass.

Tired of the magic show, Vanagor ordered the Red Hordes to destroy them all. The Hordes and the Guards clashed in the middle of the battle field. Gangus kept most of them at bay with the wind from his staff. The Shamans sent undead into the mix, but Brehira sent them crashing to the ground, and Lerayah turned them to dust.

The Hordes had never faced the likes of Dinary before and were quite surprised that they couldn't finish him off. The more the necklace glowed, the harder Dinary fought. He slashed the throat of one Horde, decapitated another and ran a third through with his mighty sword. Unafraid of their height, size, and fearsome appearance, Dinary pushed forward, slashing and cutting everything in sight. Celio and his men were right behind him, slashing and cutting those who had managed to escaped Dinary's sword.

Gangus's staff wore out. He grabbed his sword and ran into the battle to face a Horde. He fought two Hordes at a time and almost lost his life. When the Emperor spotted Gangus and saw that he could handle two of his Hordes, he became hot with anger and ordered six of his Hordes not to come back without Lord Abram's head. Gangus saw them coming and quickly came up with a strategy to even the odds in his favor. He ran and fell at the feet of one and cut his legs from under him; he jumped up and took off another's head, then quickly ran another through. One stood in front of him, another at his left side and still another behind him. Gangus turned quickly stabbed the one behind him in the groin then stood to face the two Hordes. He took on the two Hordes—slashing, cutting and stabbing until both lay at his feet, headless.

"Bloody Hell," Vanagor said under his breath. He pulled out his secret weapons, twin swords that had been blessed by Nelchael and dismounted his horse. He bolted into the field running towards Gangus.

"Lord Abram!" he shouted

Gangus turned and saw just above the heads on the blood stained field the golden skull crown with its ruby eyes rushing towards him. He watched as Vanagor came more clearly into view and advancing with swords in both hands. Vanagor stopped then walked slowly towards Gangus, and Gangus walked slowly towards him. Both stopped and faced each other. They were about ten feet apart, when Vanagor said, "This war ends now, Lord Abram."

"As you wish, Emperor."

The men raised their swords, but Brehira, who stood afar, sensed something strange about the Emperor's weapons and yelled, "Wait!" Gangus and Vanagor froze. Brehira ran out and quickly blessed Gangus' sword. "Now," she said, looking sternly at Vanagor. The Emperor realizing he no longer had the advantage, jeered at Brehira as she quickly left to join the others who stood and watched. The Nordoxz also stood silently gazing—each praying to their god for their leader. There were no shouts, no birds flying from trees, not even a stir from the wind. The sun hid behind the dark clouds as sparks shot from the first strike of the blades.

The crowd watched as the opponents—both great heights and muscular circled with their blades upheld. The Emperor charged at Gangus with his right blade with a foreswing and followed it with a backswing. Then he did the same with the left blade, foreswing then quickly with a backswing. Gangus barely dodged the left blade and met the left with a foreswing of his own. Vanagor was surprised when the weight of Gangus' blade drove him back, back, back, but not enough to knock him off balance which was what Gangus intended. Gangus smiled and made eye contact. Vanagor was impressed, but it only made him angrier, and he wasn't about to let this inferior humanoid win.

"Ahhhh," Vanagor shouted as he lunged at Gangus. Clank! Clank! Clank! The red and blue sparks lit up the space above them as their equal abilities caused each to miss flesh. "Ahhhh," Vanagor shouted as he advanced slashing Gangus' arm. Gangus staggered back as the blood dripped off his hand. Gangus lifted his blade and brought it down so hard, it drove Vanagor's heels into the mud up to his ankles. Then Gangus fell to his knees, rolled and slashed the calf of Vanagor's leg. Vanagor hopped about to gain his balance. Gangus made eye contact and smirked. The Emperor's eyes that were as black as coals bore into Gangus' eyes as he ignored his pain and charged Gangus with a vengeance. He drove Gangus back and back and back, slashing, and cutting, both swords hitting its mark so fast, Gangus was nearly beheaded twice.

Vanagor took a few seconds to catch his breath then noticed Gangus' blood-soaked garments. Vanagor grinned, but became over confident; he charged again, but Gangus dodged and stabbed the Emperor in the side, just missing his heart. Vanagor cried out and fell to one knee but managed to scramble to his feet though blood gushed from his side. Both, dripping with blood, circled with their bloody blades upheld. As sparks flew overhead, the onlookers continued to pray to their gods. When Gangus appeared to get the best of Vanagor, a Shaman gifted with summoning and controlling the undead tried to sneak one onto the field, but Lerayah spotted it and turned it to dust. The Shaman gritted his teeth at her, and she flashed him a crooked smile.

As the red and blue sparks continued to flash, both, looking beaten and bloody, battled on. Black clouds hung over the field as blades clanked again and again with no sure winner. Then Brehira and the Guards loudly gasped when Gangus lost his footing in the slippery mud and fell on his back. Vanagor ceased the opportunity. He stood over Gangus and battled him relentlessly. Dinary held his breath and nearly ran out on the field, but was held back by Brehira who knew what a lone victory could mean for her husband and his leadership. Gangus' great strength and quick-wit paid off; he slashed the left wrist of Vanagor and caused him to drop one of his swords. Then Gangus kicked Vanagor back which gave Gangus time to scramble to his feet. Vanagor's nose flared and his jaw to tighten. Gangus charged him, and the high pitch sound of the blades striking reached the throne of the gods as each had a stake in the outcome.

Vanagor, fighting on one good leg, battled Gangus to no end. *"What's holding him up?"* Vanagor thought, seething. He charged Gangus but swung wildly only nipping the top of his head. But Gangus replayed one of his strategies. He dropped to his knees, rolled and slashed the legs of the Emperor. The Nordoxz cringed as their leader crashed to the ground with no legs. He tried to stand on his bloody stumps. He lifted his sword, determined to fight to the death, but Gangus slowly walked over and kicked the blade from his hand and stood above him.

"You are right, Emperor. This war ends now." He beheaded the once invincible Emperor of the Nordoxz—a nation that had caused so much fear in Bethica and detriment to the divine gods. Gangus lifted the head on his sword to thunderous cheers from his army. The crown that Vanagor wore had long been discarded and lay somewhere upon the bloody battle field. Brehira ran out to greet him with the army right behind her.

Barthod screamed Gangus' name and fired a bolt of lightning. Brehira, caught off guard, attempted to block it, but the lightning struck her, killing her instantly.

"Brehira!" Gangus caught her before her body hit the ground. Celio tried to revive her, but his power was not strong enough to resurrect.

"Mother!" Dinary screamed. He turned to charge the Shaman but stopped short when the sky turned black with large flesh eating birds. They were known to pick a large mammal's bones clean in seconds. Controlled by Olutunji, hundreds of them swooped down, their teeth sharp as steel blades, the Shamans tried to cast a spell, but the birds quickly devoured them—leaving behind skull and bones. Barthod was the only Shaman left. He threw lightning at the birds and kept them at bay, thinking he had escaped his fellow Shaman's fate. But Olutunji had given the bird's instruction and had saved Barthod for himself. While Barthod was preoccupied throwing lightning bolts at the birds, Olutunji shapeshifted into a Mastodon, a wooly-haired giant elephant with three feet tusk. He charged Barthod, stabbing him again and again with his tusk and impaling him. He shook Barthod off his tusk then fell upon him, while he was yet alive, and crushed him. Barthod screamed, and his eyes popped out of his head; blood and guts oozed from his body and mingled with the mud on the ground.

After shapeshifting back into humanoid form, Olutunji ran to Brehira and kneeled beside her. He held her hand and wept. Celio had to pull him away from her and off the field.

Throughout Bethica, Gangus was hailed as a hero, but he was in no mood for celebration. The love of his life was gone from him forever. Brehira was buried under her favorite shade tree overlooking a beautiful lake that was re-named for her.

As for the Nordoxz, without their Emperor or Shamans, they disappeared from Bethica.

*****

High on Mount Zunus, the gods gathered for a victory celebration. Earlier, thundering voices marked the exile of Nelchael, god of death when evidence of his involvement in the dark forces behind the Nordoxz proved irrefutable. While falling to Hades, Nelchael's booming voice echoed his revenge.

The gods sat on their thrones exquisitely attired in fine linen and jeweled crowns. Modiah, the goddess of dance sat playing a lyre accompanying ballerinas and a fifty-player chorus. The chorus repeated lines written by the goddess of epics that detailed the dramatic actions of Gangus from the mighty winds of his staff to the beheading of the Emperor of the Nordoxz.

The music flowed as each deity declared arrogantly that their forces played the major role in saving Bethica. Goddess Dahlia gave credit to the Dedroyles and the gifts she bestowed upon Brehira. Stating that she had rewarded Lady Abram with immortality and a castle in Elysium to await Gangus' immortal soul.

"Bah!" Gailzur bellowed. "The Drake would have burned Lord Abram to a crispy snack if it had not been for Celio's Sheild."

"Ha!"Zakzakiel snapped. "And what about my Fighting Machine? Have you ever seen anything to match Dinary?"

"Oh, yes," Dahlia said pretending to yawn. "Your little silver trinket with the emerald eyes. I almost forgot."

"Trinket!?" Zakakiel said. "Dahlia, you *are* funny?"

"Can't we even celebrate without arguing, Raziel pleaded. "Listen, let's say Lord Abrams is a cake. Now, a cake needs important ingredients. Otherwise, it isn't a cake." The goddess, Zakakiel, and Gailzur looked at Raziel puzzlingly. "But," Raziel continued, "you wouldn't put candles on flour, or butter or honey, or a dish of milk. You'd put the candles on the cake."

"I think your explanation is silly," Zakakiel said, "but we get your meaning."

"Good, then we all agree this is Lord Abram's celebration. So, let us lift our cups?" Raziel said lifting his jewel goblet. The goddess and the two gods lifted their goblets and drank to Lord Gangus Abram.

The celebration continued as all agreed that Gangus deserved the highest praise. Dahlia patted her feet to the music; Raziel clapped along, while Gailzur and Zakzakiel tried to over shout each other singing the Ballard of the Mighty Gangus song. But as time wore on, Raziel found that he was back to refereeing as the threesome slowly gravitated to who did the most to add Gangus in his victory.

The Chronicles of Bethica

"Brehira, and shut up!"
"Dinary, and *you* shut up!"

Chapter Twenty

The Angel of Light

Lord Gangus Abram was a hundred and four. Many claimed he bore the blessings of his god. Although his hair was white like sheep's wool, his back was as straight as any man's half his age, and his eyes were as clear as an eagle's. His body shone many scars from battles; the deadliest he'd sustained in the Great War against the Nordoxz. And as it was the custom of his tribe, Lord Abram sat in the midst of his tribesman to recite the history of his people to a new generation. The large fire crackled, and sparks dispersed into the night air like red fireflies. Never tiring of the stories, the adults settled back with a smile as the children's eyes focused on the lips of this great monarch, as he began the second of two stories; this one more closely to his heart.

"They once said of me," Gangus began, *"that I was a man of great courage. I was revered for my faith in our god and my obedience to his will. But I can't take credit for that. Who wouldn't live or die for such a god as the one I serve?*

I lived many years in a land that had no name. The land had existed uninhabited for so long that the name was forgotten. Finally, we called the land Volaria, after my father's race. It was truly a paradise, and the land yielded abundantly: there were fruit trees and vast gardens as far as the eye could see. The lakes overflowed with every kind of edible creature, and the weather was always favorable. Now, I know this will be hard for you to believe, but there was no sickness in our bodies or our minds; no hatred or bitterness towards our brethren; and all Volarians dealt fairly with one another."

"Then, why would you leave such a splendid land, Lord Abram?" one bright-eyed boy asked as he sat cross-legged in the inner circle with the other children.

"Well, little one," he said with a smile, *"I was awakened one night by a mysterious voice. It was like no other voice I had ever heard. It spoke boastfully, yet, in a whisper; it came from everywhere, yet nowhere could I pinpoint it. It reeked with such authority that I had to obey.*

'Rise quickly,' the voice said, 'and seek a man called Naman who lives at the north end of the forest. There, you will find a single cottage.' So, I rose and dressed, grabbed my

cloak and a lantern and headed for the north end of the forest.

"Were you frightened?" His eight-year-old great, great, granddaughter asked.

"*Let's just say old Great Grand was as scared as a caterpillar riding the back of a Bay Bird,*" he said with a chuckle. The children giggled and squirmed.

One of Gangus' great granddaughters stood. "Great Grandfather, I do apologize, but it is time for the little ones to be in bed."

"No! No!" the children yelled one by one.

"Now, now children, I promise I will tell more of the story during the Bull feast," Gangus said.

The children, with their sad faces, were led single-file out of camp and into their various homes and were the servants prepared them for bed.

*****

Later that night, Gangus knelt beside his bed and prayed. He gave thanks for his sons, Khimah and Dinary. Dinary had two sons, Glinas and Petruss. Petruss, the eldest had five daughters. Glinas, the youngest had two wives and twelve sons who headed the twelve kingdoms of the Abramites. Inspired by the visions god had given him, Glinas directed each of his sons to erect a city using indigenous servants and to live there with their children, making them the first Lords of each new empire.

After finishing his prayer, Gangus climbed into bed and pulled the covers up to his chin. He felt the empty pillar next to him—the place where his beloved had once slept. He never remarried, though he could have. But who could replace such a jewel as Brehira? How he missed her. Gangus shifted his body beneath the covers. He grabbed the pillar that the servants always sprinkled with Brehira's scented oils and pressed it to his chest. He slept with it, as he usually did, all night.

*****

Early the next morning, Gangus was rudely awakened by screams and shouts. He grabbed a cloak, and in his bare feet ran across to the window to peer out. What he saw was chaos among his people. The Bohaus had entered the land and were killing the livestock. Since left behind by the defeated Nordoxz, the Bohaus had no masters and were left to wander and pillage.

For several years, they had become a threat to many small villages and cities throughout the region. But this was their first time they had invaded the Abramatic region. These creatures proved a deadly nuisance, killing off farmer's herds, wildlife, and even domestic animals were not safe.

Gangus, half dressed and in sandals, ran outside with his sword. His son, grandsons and fellow clansmen had steered many of the herds of cattle, sheep, horses, and mules into the barns and were standing guard. Gangus slashed one of the Bohaus, severing its spine then finishing it off with a stab through the eye. He slashed several times at another, cutting off its head.

Every soldier's sword was bloody, and fifty to sixty Bohaus lay dead. Still more crowded into the area where soldiers stood with weapons ready. They attacked, and swords were swishing in every direction. Heads, huge legs and other body parts of the beasts flew up into the air. Still, the Bohaus kept coming.

Then something that Gangus had never witnessed. These creatures showed some intelligence. They appeared to be communicating with one that appeared bigger than them all. A few scurried out of view. Everyone looked at each other and gazed at their surroundings. Then suddenly, Bohaus appeared on top of the roofs of houses and barns.

"My god," Gangus said. "These beasts are planning to dive on us."

"Don't worry, Grandfather. I have an idea." Glinas yelled and pointed to several soldiers. "Get into formation."

The men scrambled and stood beneath the roofs, looking up at the creatures.

"Don't lift your weapons until I tell you!" Glinas shouted.

The Bohaus moved in from the front, sides, and rear, while those on the roofs lowered their heads and bore their sharp fangs. A hundred soldiers faced the creatures from the front. Another hundred and ten faced them at the rear, and fifty to sixty stood looking up at the roofs.

Life grew still as if nature itself had braced for the attack. There were no birds flying overhead; no small creatures scattering to and foe; not even an insect was in motion; no one moved—the creatures stood like statues as if they were waiting for a sign. Then, the alpha beast stood on three hind legs with three pointing upward and let out a deep growl that sounded like thunder and that nearly shattered the ears of every Volarian. With acid dripping from their fangs, the beasts leaped from every roof top.

"NOW!" Glinas shouted. Sixty to seventy spears shot upward as the beast fell on top of them. Some that were impaled still managed to tear off the faces and heads of their captors. Other creatures managed to miss the spear, and had squashed the men so deeply into the earth that the place where they lay became their shallow grave. Screams from soldiers rose into the air as the acid dissolved them alive. Only skeletons with swords gripped in their bony fingers remained.

The Bohaus moved in from the front, sides, and rear. The brave soldier's blades were tearing into the beasts from all angles; their blades flashing so fast, they looked like the sparkles of stars in a day sky. Blood covered Gangus from head to foot as he drove his blade again and again; gutting and beheading and downing one beast after another at his feet. There were shouts and death cries and growls and howling from Bohaus that were injured. There were screams from the children who were hidden and protected; but nothing could protect them from the sounds they heard coming from the outside where their fathers and grandfathers, brothers and uncles were all engaged in a battle for their lives.

Suddenly and without warning, the great alpha Bohaus roared, but it sounded different—higher pitched than before. The beasts froze, then turned and retreated. Badly wounded with ears, eyes, and limbs missing, the Bohaus fled into a thickly wooded area and disappeared.

The Volarian men gave a great shout that scattered the birds out of the top of trees, their blood-dripping swords and spears held upward in victory.

"They'll be back; god help us," Gangus said.

"And we'll be ready for them Father," Dinary answered with a smirk.

The women emerged out of hiding with the children in tow; they cheered their men while the children wiped the tears from their eyes—seeing that many of their fathers were alive. But the tears soon returned with the death count of the clansmen who had so bravely fallen. It took an entire day to load and haul away all the dead Bohaus and body parts, and to prepare the fallen clansmen for burial. Gangus prayed to his god—asking that the fallen men share a glorious place in his mighty kingdom then he ate, drank and re- tired to his bed chamber.

Weeks later, at the annual Bull Feast, the children were all perked and ready for more of Gangus' story; they gathered in an inner circle, their little ears waiting and their bright eyes on Lord Abrams' lips.

Let me see, Gangus pondered, pulling on his snow white beard and pretending his head was fuzzy. The old trickster, he never forgot a thing. He had many stories in his head and could recite them all as accurately as the day they had happened. *Oh, yes*, he said sticking his index finger in the air, *with map in hand, I left the blind Oracle Naman and returned home....*

*****

There were many other celebrations during that year, one being the holiest celebration of the Abramites, called Mashubah, a seven-day feast worshipping their god for nothing more than his being holy and righteous. For seven days they'd refrain from asking their god for anything—for it would be selfish and would negate the whole purpose of their worship.

There were much food and wine. The women wore long, sleeveless white tunics with gold jewelry. The men wore short-sleeved, royal blue, togas that came at the knee with thin, gold sashes around their waists; their swords were shined to perfection and worn in leather sheaths decorated with Old World markings. There was laughter and dancing and games. Young boys hunted small harmless rodents with their play bow and arrows, a game that in the following years would aid them during real training in hunting Redhawks, a stable diet of the tribe.

Gangus took a jug of wine and walked away from the cheerful crowd. He had always enjoyed taking a stroll through the tall piper lilies and watched the silver jumping fish hop out of the water and gulp down flying insects. He sipped from the jug, and then lay back on the blue-green grass and closed his eyes, unaware that just a hundred feet away, he was being watched by an assassin. Seven feet tall, over two hundred pounds and wearing a skeletal mask, he lifted his sword as he crept upon Gangus.

A young boy who had chased his little prey nearby saw the masked stranger and yelled, "Lord Abram, look out!"

Gangus eyes flashed open just in time to roll out of the way as the sword thundered down upon the spot where he had lain. He pulled his sword from his side but wasn't able to get a clean shot at the man. The assassin swung the blade at Gangus' face several times but had missed attempts to cut off his head. Gangus took advantage of his being shorter than the Assassin and swung his blade at his knee, slicing into it. The assassin growled as he went down. Gangus slashed off his ear then leaped upon him—straddling him and lifting his sword to stab his chest, but the assassin knocked him off and quickly scrambled to his feet. Gangus hopped to his feet. Both resumed a fighting stance and began to circle. Gangus wielded his sword that was met by the assassin's blade. It was steel against steel. The light from the sun bounced off the striking blades as they clanked and sparked. Neither showed fear nor seemed willing to relent.

The tip of the assassin's blade slashed Gangus' cheek as he avoided yet another attempt by the assassin to behead him. The assassin swung again, but Gangus ducked causing the assassin to lose his balance and step awkwardly into Gangus' swing of his blade which took off the assassin's hand. Blood poured from the stump. But to Gangus' surprise, the Assassin switched his blade to the other hand and drove it into Gangus' heart.

The young boy came running ahead of Dinary, Glinas and his men.

"Father!" Dinary yelled, his eyes fixed upon Gangus' breathless body.

"No!" Glinas said his eyes glassy. "Attack!" he yelled to his men in a screeching voice. But a blinding light from the sky caused them to halt and shield their eyes. It lingered for a moment then two pairs of transparent wings sprang from the light. It had arms and what resembled a body and a head, but no face. A stream of light was where legs and feet might have been. When the assassin looked up at it, he screamed as his eyes melted out of his head and blood and tiny pieces of brain matter spilled through the sockets. He fell to his knees and turned to ashes. Then the light reached down, scooped up Gangus' body and shot up to the sky—zig zagging like a deflated balloon and disappeared into the blue.

Dinary couldn't close his mouth. All of the men stood gazing up at the sky. Glinas' knees went weak, and he had to be caught by two of his men.

"Holy god of the universe. What was that?" one of the men blurted.

"Where did it take him?" asked another.

Then Dinary found his voice. "What do we tell the others? No one's going to believe us," he said. "Especially since everyone knows we've drunk much wine."

"They'll believe '*me*,'" said a voice above them. The men looked up and saw a man standing majestically and holding a gold staff. The man stared without looking at them.

The Chronicles of Bethica

"Who are you?" Dinary asked.

"I am Naman, the Oracle your father spoke off." Then he disappeared as quickly as he had appeared.

Dinary and Glinas looked puzzling at one another; then both ran to where the Light had snatched Gangus up. There, on the ground laid the assassin's severed gloved hand. Glinas stooped, picked it up and removed the glove.

Dinary, taken aback, noticed the humanoid hand with skin spotted like an animal. "No," he said looking over Glinas' shoulder. "Nordoxz?"

*****

For many years, the story of Gangus and the Angel of Light rang out in poems, songs, and plays throughout the land. One late evening, as servants packed away Lord Abram's belongings, they discovered three very large books—all in brown leather bindings, that appeared hidden away among his things in an old trunk. One of the books, in particular, marked Rise of the Nordoxz, intrigued them. They took the books to Glinas.

When Glinas received the books, he appeared delighted. Many generations had heard Gangus tell the story of his coming to this land, but never had he gone into details about the notorious Nordoxz, the tribe that had struck terror in the hearts of Bethicans. Some said just the name alone seemed enough to send trembles up one's spine. Tales of the Nordoxz got played out in children's nightmares. One night while all slept, Glinas opened one of the books, Dawn of the Nordoxz, and read the first lines.

Ages ago, in the royal land of Bore, there reigned a mighty Dragon queen who lost everything she loved to war—

About The Author

Warren W. Randall Jr. is an RPG game designer and System Administrator for a global Pennsylvania company. A native of Baltimore, Warren now lives in Alliance, Ohio with his beautiful wife, Diana, and stepson Jonathan. His passion for RPG flows through every page of The Chronicles of Bethica from the richness of his characters to his exquisite imagination in every battle scene.

Warren also runs gaming sessions at least twice a month. His new RPG book, The Realm of Bethica has been praised by Pittsburgh and Ohio gamers a like and will soon hit shelves and online book stores. New books from his trilogy, Dawn of the Nordoxz and Rise of the Nordoxz will be released in the not too distant future. Please visit the website realmofbethica.com for more information about this talented author.

www.ingramcontent.com/pod-product-compliance
Lightning Source LLC
Chambersburg PA
CBHW061214170626
46809CB00003B/1348